COIN FOREMAN
COULD NOT HELP BUT GROW UP

Both of his parents were dead. He and his sisters had been left under the tutelage of a brutal, twisted guardian in the hell of a Brooklyn slum. He had been tossed into the middle of life without having tasted its pleasures or its joys.

Escape meant the Navy, Italy, and the kind of adventures in love, friendship, and uninhibited sexuality that Coin had never even read about, let alone experienced.

"MR. DODSON DOES NOT SPARE HIS READERS . . . HE WRITES WITH POWER."
—*Christian Science Monitor*

COME HOME EARLY, CHILD

Owen Dodson

POPULAR LIBRARY • NEW YORK

POPULAR LIBRARY EDITION
January, 1977

Copyright © 1977 by Owen Dodson

ISBN: 0-445-08549-5

For my sister
Edith

For without a cement of blood (it must be human, it must be innocent) no secular wall will safely stand.

—W. H. Auden
Vespers

Chapter One

The night Coin Foreman was returned home from
his wanderings, the Corinthian Baptist Church of
Christ burned to the ground in a five-alarm fire.
Along Berriman Street the news was flashed from
open window to open window by popped-out heads
and mouths and mouths working into the disaster
gossip like fast scissors.

"Been burning now for close to three hours, say
half the fire brigades of Brooklyn working on
it. . . ."

"And that ain't all. They broadcasting the evacu-
ation for three blocks around."

"Almost started to join that church but something told me, something said right out loud. . . ."

". . . and they're calling on Manhattan to get to
the rescue. . . ."

"I knew something was gonna happen when
them church collections was stolen. . . ."

On the sidewalk Mrs. Fox and Mrs. Carth

nodded together: chickens picking corn, Coin thought, as he watched.

"It's the vengeance of God on them," panted Mrs. Carth.

"The insurance, I hope the insurance is paid," answered Mrs. Fox.

The Richardsons and the Jefferses had stopped playing bridge and carried the news from group to group. They were flyer pigeons roosting on the faraway siren calls and now flying away to excite other air with news.

"They telephone me," cried Mrs. Jeffers, "that a dead body's lying at the pulpit like a roast."

"O Great Savior," was all Mrs. Richardson could manage.

"Cyril," yelled Mrs. Jeffers to her husband, "didn't I tell you about them cigarettes? Put that one out this minute."

"Woman, I been smoking since I was a child in Trinidad."

Mrs. Jeffers was beside herself. "Cyril, I said put that damn cigarette out."

The children had stopped playing catch and jumping rope, and take-a-giant-step. They begged to go to the fire of their lives. No parent said yes and a clamor went up.

Coin was hurried along by Miss Lucy Horwitz. They were chased down the street by the darkness, in and out of spotlight street lamps. The scissor talk made wounds in Coin's aching head. He was safe now and at home and unhappy. His church was burning down, not the synagogue or St. Gabriel's but his church. No one had greeted or recognized him or said I'm sorry, Coin. Miss Horwitz had her hand nailed to his; she wasn't going to take any chances that he'd run away again while he was with *her*.

"You'd better stay with me, boy. We don't want any more criminals in the family like your brother Oscar. Well, they can shout their prayers in the gutters now for all I care. I only hope Agnes doesn't get too close to that heat. I told her not to go there tonight but oh, no, your father just dragged her along to that funeral as if she hasn't had funerals enough."

Mrs. Renaldo was coming toward them in her usual mourning clothes.

"Gracious, here comes that Italian scarecrow. Probably got liquor on her breath. I hate liquor, anyhow. Let's cross over." Coin pulled back.

Mrs. Renaldo had already reached them with her half-dragging trot. She stumbled toward Coin, her love for him spread out in those arms. She hugged him away from Miss Horwitz: *"O mio angelo, o mio angelo,* Coin. Where? Where? Where were you lost? I missed, I missed, I missed you every day."

Coin stayed in her arms. It was his first welcome home, even if she was rocking with chianti wine and dug her nails into his shoulder blades. Coin loved her. She had been his mother's friend. Miss Horwitz jerked him out of the clamping embrace.

Now he was forced to go to the fire where he really wanted to go. But he wanted to stay, too, closed in those black sleeves of love.

During the short ride on the El, toward the scene of the fire, Miss Horwitz talked as always, sharp, as if she wanted to puncture the tire of a boy's bike.

"That Mrs. Renaldo's always hugging people. You'd better watch out, Coin, one of these days you'll get a disease. I hate people to be feeling of me, anyhow."

Coin was looking out of the window near Troy Avenue. He wasn't studying her a bit; he was thinking of all the other rides he had taken along this same route with his brother Woody and his sister Bernice and his father chewing gum to disguise the cigar smell. He was thinking of the morning he became a Christian so that he could pray for his mother to get well and. . . . He was thinking of the pennies he had stolen from the collection plate to spite God because his mother had died anyway. He had had his enemies and the chief one was God. . . . He had started his revenge the Sunday after the funeral when the usher passed that old red velvet collection plate. And every time he took out a penny one of God's white hairs fell. Old baldyheaded God. So after a while he took to drinking lots of water. He wasn't scared now about his sin because he had nothing to do with this fire. A year ago he would have wallowed in ashes like the Jews in their grief and atonement. He was a wanderer when it all started. It wasn't his fire.

"Coin, are you listening to what I'm saying?"

"Yes, Miss Horwitz."

"What did I say just now?"

"I don't know; it's so hot in here I'd like to die."

"Where did you get that expression from? From some of your friends on the road?"

She made "road" and "friends" sound like they were the backside of nothing. She bared her purple gums, letting out the smell of old mayonnaise. Her hand was still nailed to his; the sweat between their palms was anchor glue. His "friends on the road." After he had sneaked away from his blind Uncle Troy and his girl friend, Mrs. Walker, who made his uncle do dirty things in bed in Washington, D.C., he got on a train for Kentucky with his saved-up money to find his only new friend, Ferris. He didn't even know Ferris's last name, but only that he lived in a town that began with the three letters M A D . . . and that in Ferris's house was a golden synagogue chair. Ferris had said, "If you come visit me, Coin, you can take it back for your father to sit in." And then Ferris had laughed his honeysuckle laugh and continued, "If you really came, I'd like to die." He remembered that when he had entered that train for Ferris's Kentucky, every coach was crowded, loud with noise and funky. As he would pass through with his excuse-mes, people turned to stare at him with his greasy lunch bag and the tag on his chest:

9

COIN FOREMAN—TEN YEARS OLD

I am going to Madison, Kentucky—To me met
    by Ferris
In case of accident of death get in touch with
    Ferris

Nobody had bothered to read it, not even the lady
at the ticket place. She had looked at it but didn't
bother to read. He had printed it nice, copying
from the tag his sister Agnes had put on him when
he first started for D.C., and changing it to suit
himself. And he carried his map, too. The one
bought at Union Station souvenir counter. He had
spread it out on a bench real smooth and found
Kentucky way over there. How many mountains
there were to cross, the rivers and cities, the lines
on all the plains. And the crisscrossing lines. With
his greasy bag, to Mad—spelled Madison—his fat
hope. He knew where he was going. But Ferris
would be at the end. He was put in mind of the
clown with the white face, red hearts painted on his
cheeks and a smile painted on purple, a wig the
color of carrots in his father's backyard. The old
clown danced on, pulling at a peppermint rope. He
pulled and he pulled for all he was worth and the
rope never stopped coming, it kept on coming until
the middle ring of the circus was filled with the
candy colors ... finally at the end there came a
prancing juggler tossing golden balls with lights on

them. He kept seven going like magic. That's how he knew it was going to be with him on the train; Ferris would be at the finish.

So he hadn't minded the stares. He was bunked from side to side by the people and the movement of the train until he reached the last car. Here there was silence except for shifting feet and bags being thunked on overhead racks. Everyone seemed to move around as in a silent movie while the train pushed toward Kentucky with buopola, buopola, buopola music. Wheels of music. He found a seat near a hot window and sat up tall for a while. In a minute he was slumped down and asleep. He woke up with a start. It was dark outside. Pebbles of summer rain beat against his window. For a moment he didn't know where he was: at church weeping as he looked at his mother in the coffin, leading his blind Uncle Troy around Washington, D.C., or with Ferris gathering apples from his golden garden in Kentucky. He felt as if he was stuffed in a bag of straw and couldn't breathe. When he looked around he felt cross-eyed like the time he was first drunk in the Jim-Jam Cafe in D.C. Next to him was a lump-of-dough man, fast asleep, working spit in the corners of his lips, one hand between his legs, resting on a long lump in his pants, and the other on Coin's thigh. He dared not move. There were still wheels of music but the sound was slippery in the rain. A scream in his throat was like to explode in a fire engine sound; he smelled old mayonnaise.

11

The man at his side shifted awake. He poked his tongue at Coin and conjured signals with his fingers into his face. Still there was no sound. Coin put his fingers into his ears to see if they were stopped up. He looked around, afraid. He longed to vanish back into his crocus sack of straw. But he couldn't get in again. When he looked around the whole car was filled to bursting with the people making their fingers in signs, pursing their lips, stretching their mouths at each other, rolling their heads, scratching the air. The only sound was slippery in the rain. He was fully awake now. Suddenly it dawned on him that they were talking in semaphore. Giant puppet men. He doubted if he could ever speak again and he was afraid to try. The man next to him rubbed Coin's sweating head. Kept rubbing and bubbling with his mouth sliding back and forth on a harmonica of air. Coin managed to say a scared hello. But the man gestured more than ever. Once, long ago, when he couldn't answer one of Miss Raidin's questions in school, she had asked him if he was deaf and dumb. Now he whispered as if he were dazed awake: yes, Miss Raidin, I'm deaf and dumb, I'm deaf and dumb, I'm deaf and dumb . . . bell. That did it. He could move now. He shook his head free of the scratching hand. They all looked toward him and he smiled and made little motions with his mouth and tried to talk with his hands. A carload of smiles turned in his direction. Soon he heard crackling paper and smelled food. He remembered his lunch clutched in his hand nearest the window.

As he started to open it a gentle hand took it from him and thrust a chicken leg at him; others came over with rolls or a piece of fruit or half a sandwich. They smiled and urged him to eat by eating themselves and pointing to the food they had offered. It was a different kind of picnic from the annual ones given by the Sunday School of the Corinthian Baptist Church on Bear Mountain; these faces around him were just as happy, with him in the center. If Ferris was here it would be complete. He stuffed himself, grinning around between fast bites at his silent-talking Santa Clauses.

When the conductor came for the tickets, Coin fished his out and waited. Maybe this was where he would be caught or asked questions he couldn't answer. But with his friends in the car and the food peaceful inside him, he wasn't afraid. Starting from the far end of the car he heard the bite of the puncher into tickets. He was almost the last. The big human blue wall was beside him, examined his ticket, his tag, and then his face. Coin wiped at the grease around his mouth. The silent friends began to creep close, making a circle, when the conductor said that he was sorry but Coin didn't belong in this car.

"You belong in the first car, sonny, near where the engine is at." And he started to lift Coin by his arm. What did he do that for? The circle with the freak wavings, the harmonica-playing mouths, the extra spit, the crazy semaphore, closed around the conductor and walked him toward the door. Blue

13

wall stopped near the door. Everyone else stopped, too. Blue wall shot his arm out, pointed his finger, like a Keystone traffic cop in the movies, directly at Coin.

"Sonny, I'm telling you, this car ain't for colored!" He shut the door with a soft swish and was gone.

An arrow had been aimed at Coin and shot. The deaf and dumb were moving toward him to ease it out.

"Coin," Miss Horwitz was saying, "have you lost your senses? Don't you know where to get off after all these years?"

Coin stumbled out with his mind still stretched into the past. It wasn't until they were on the street that he was jerked back to the present by the fire engines clanging, flashing their murder-red lights, the siren sounds cutting the hot blue-serge air, Miss Horwitz talking to herself and him at once, enjoying ahead of time the piles of ashes and bricks they were to see. Her body looked carved out of a mass of brown shoe polish, as matter-of-fact as a shoelace, her eyes were shining.

"Come on, Coin, stop dawdling along, you'll have plenty of time for that when your sister Agnes slaps you unconscious for worrying everybody to death. Running away from your uncle like you didn't have the sense you were born with!"

They didn't have the sense they were born with, farming him out to lead around a drunken blind man who spent most of his time playing the numbers and feeling up Mrs. Walker. He wondered why his sister Agnes skipped around Miss Mayonnaise-smelling Horwitz, when she was so cross all the time and walked as if she always had the bathroom on her mind. She was looking at him now, reading his mind probably. Flushing his thoughts.

"Coin, you look like you've been starved to death. On the way home we'll stop by the Y. W. C. A. and get something good to eat. And I have some candy in my room. That might sweeten that sour face of yours."

Just when he was beginning to hate her she got so nice an all-day lollypop would dissolve in her mouth. I bet she doesn't have peppermint as long as the clown's rope. And he laughed to himself.

"Would you like that?"

"Yes, Miss Horwitz."

"Now we're getting somewhere," and she squeezed the sweat of her palm into his, making a sucking sound. If she'd only let his hand go. He was always being caught, trapped.

"We'd better go to Fort Green Park and look from there. I suppose Agnes went there with the others. No use in us getting burned, is there? And *you'll* be able to see everything. I'm not walking you too fast, am I? You're a big boy now, almost a young man. We want to get there before it's all over, you know, before they put it out."

She was talking in short pants. She seemed to want to run. She even let go of his hand in her hurry. She was almost laughing like the old sisters laughed in church when God won sinners.

"Coin, you're going to miss it," and she snatched up his hand again.

She's happy because there's burning down, she offered me candy because there's terrible. She's even running like a little girl for a favorite doll. The thoughts rammed into his head, from where he'd never know.

As they rapidly climbed the hill of the park to the lookout, gazing east Coin saw the puffing smoke lined with murder-red, and straight ahead on the lookout, everywhere, crowds of people strained in one direction toward the burning place where they once had praised the Lord. He was sweaty hot but shivered cold as they passed group after group. Miss Horwitz smiled now and again to people she knew. No one smiled back or even noticed. Only the sound of fire laughing in nanny goat sounds, sneezing, harking, spitting, biting the air for food. On a high rock stood Reverend Brooks, hands behind his back like a prisoner waiting for the noose (he had preached his mother's funeral: "I am the resurrection and the life and the light. . . . She is not sealed in this coffin, she has already arisen and is in our midst like a star to guide us. Naomi Starr Foreman . . .") or a statue prophet doomsday couldn't melt. Next to him was his mother's old nurse, Mrs. Quick, who had urged him to become a Christian so that he could pray for his mother to get well. (She had said to him before his mother went to the faith healer to be cured of her paralysis: "Then the needy brings up their affliction and they kneels down and he prays for each and every one separate and they think real deep on the Lord. Many rise up well and cured."

"Is Mama? . . ." he had asked in that long ago.

"Your mother's got the strength and faith to remove mountains." His mother was dead but Mrs. Quick was still on the Lord's side. Coin moved away from her.

Whole walls of the church had been eaten by fire. Where they were not all gone they looked like his brother Oscar's teeth: yellow, scarred black, uneven. Where the firemen had sprayed the most water, the charcoal wood and mess of seat cushions and hymnals reminded him of lakes of pus. The back wall, where the pulpit was, hadn't fallen yet and the steeple and the dead clock near the top stayed steady. Sometimes the wind blew clouds of smoke away suddenly, showing a blooming moon and summer stars, and then blew the smoke back into place. The hide-and-seek game.

At Coin's right was a group in black. The women had long veils. The men with them wouldn't watch down there. They seemed both alone and together, shaking with tears. Once in a while they shifted position in a losing game of wet checkers. Coin watched Mrs. Quick move toward him—there was no escape—looking like she had lost her smelling salts and ointments for those in distress. Her face was pocked in balls of sweat and her hair under the nurse's cap had gone completely back into the grease that had made it straight. She came forth whispering hoarse, her big bosoms pushing the air toward him in heat.

"Lord have mercy, here's my boy again, now you know it is." Her bosoms hit him in the nose like hot, damp suns. "Oh gracious, Coin, you done come back. Ain't that wonderful, now you know it is, that's the family of Deaconess Westerfield over there, where you been, well, pain like this come but once, leastwise I hope."

Coin started to jerk away.

"Don't be frightened, just remember your prayers. Good evening, Miss Horwitz; Coin, I'm glad your mother ain't here to witness, you know I am."

Don't mention, please don't mention my mother, please, please.

"I seen your father over yonder with Agnes." Coin was looking off. "Coin, your father's over there with your sister Agnes and Woody and Bernice; ain't this something, though."

Someone said a loud shhhhhhh shhhhhhh. Mrs. Quick took Coin to one side breathing loudly, like his father's indigestion or pleurisy, and whispering.

"You remember Deaconess Westerfield don't you, Coin? Remember how nice she was when you went up to the Christian test?"

Coin nodded without thinking.

"Well Lord, she's in that coffin there, in that fire burning up, now you know she is. I saw her laid out and I saw them close the lid and she's in there.

Oh yes. On the side, she told me she wanted the cremation even if she was a Christian. Her folks refused the request but the Lord moved in the mysterious way."

She was almost weeping now. "She were my best friend. . . ."

Voices let out shhhhhhh shhhhhhs, and Mrs. Quick shut her mouth in sucking sobs.

Miss Horwitz said, "Mrs. Quick, do you want some of your smelling salts? Get yourself together. You're not burning up or dying." Coin couldn't make out if she was making fun or trying to help Mrs. Quick.

Mrs. Quick faced Miss Horwitz direct. "Oh Lord, that this awful thing should happen to my dear Westerfield. She were born between Gemini and Cancer. And the book say she had to die this sort of way. Now you know, I don't believe that."

Miss Horwitz scanned her like she would a piece of old bacon. "Mrs. Quick, you're making everybody nervous. Please stop now."

"I'm trying, I'm trying the best I can, but it all shakes me into the marrow of my bones. I'm trying, trying. . . ."

A rocket of fire shot up, bursting in the air like Fourth of July. Red stars came down. Heads followed the design. Coin closed his eyes, wishing it would all stop and leave him in peace. He remembered touching Deaconess Westerfield's hump for good luck all those times in church. "If you touch the hump on her back it will bring you good luck, you know that," Woody had said. Coin had touched it. He was afraid now because that hump on her back didn't save her from dying double like this. Esther, his girl friend, told him that humps were like Pandora's box, filled with germs enough to kill the world. He wondered, with a shudder, if the flames would kill all the stuff in the hump or if even now the air was filled with the diseases of the world. This air smelled from everywhere, from tears to sweat, bowel movements, dead flowers, iodine, sewers, Oscar's feet, everything. He began to run and ran smack into Miss Horwitz who set her nails into his shoulders and commanded, "Stand still. Where do you think you're running to now?" There were thousands of inches of smell and disease. The wind lifted it up in a giant cloud of smoke and blew it against the crowd. The congregation faced around together, covering their faces. What Esther said couldn't be true or Miss Horwitz wouldn't be there, and if all the people believed it they must want to die because without their church they couldn't live. If everybody died Coin wanted to die, too. Except for Ferris. Coin was mixed up. So much happened at once.

The wind blew in another direction so the people could look again. New sirens began to sound, water exploded more fire into the air, worse than before, and the back wall began to crack in a lightning zigzag. A moaning went up and out of it, one voice fluttered in a bird-singing, another added to it. The dust flew out thin and clear against the cracking-wall sound, the heavy breathing of the people around him, his own loud heart, the dying of the sirens as they came to rest.

Oh, what a morning,
Ohoo, what a morning,
Ohoooo, what a morning
When the stars began to fall. . . .

Coin looked out over Brooklyn with Mrs. Quick's sobbing in the back of his head, touching his hair and his skull, working his brains. People were singing under the dust, singing within a mattress of dust. He saw way over the lights of Manhattan the Brooklyn Bridge drawn across the air above the river. There were cars everywhere, hurrying as if nothing at all was burning here. The Paramount and the Fox theaters had big signs made of millions of electric bulbs blinking off and on, announcing cowboy pictures and kissing in the tunnels of love. A zeppelin floated over the East River where every star was clear. Could the people on it see where God was burning down the history of his confession, his lessons in Matthew, Mark, Luke, and John? A third voice braided the black hairs of the song.

Ohooooooo, what a morning
When the sun refuse to shine
When the moon begins to fall

21

When the stars don't shine at all
Look in my God's right hand
When the sun begin to fall. . . .

The baptismal pool was dry.

"There ain't no use crying over spilt milk," he heard Miss Horwitz whisper to the sobbing Mrs. Quick, "look at those people down there in the streets by the church. They're moving out of their homes where they sleep and eat. Maybe all their stuff will be burned. Cry over them."

Coin hadn't noticed the streets around the church. Sure enough, families in houses across the streets on either side of the church were carrying out possessions in a hurry. Great, big, busy ants of people scurrying with mattresses rolled on their heads, bedclothes, kettles, chairs, birdcages (the birds must be dead already; no more canary songs in those houses); dogs followed their masters barking, kids had their skates and jump ropes, dolls, little suitcases; an old woman was hugging a dressmaker's dummy, dismantled beds, one woman had all her hats on her head on top of each other. A red rose bobbed on top. And the procession of those escaping was increasing, reminding him of his father's Bible story of the flight into Egypt.

"Sodom and Gomorrah!" he heard Miss Horwitz say.

Mrs. Quick was on her feet now, looking hard, with smelling salts to her nose. "Now, you know, there's Mrs. Nattie Carrington trying to sneak out of Dr. Bullock's in her underclothes, and he been a widower, lo, these many years. There's that Marshall child in a pink satin kimono escaping with the Link boy. You're right, Miss Horwitz, it ain't only the church, it's the scandal. Well, I declare! I knew the Lord must'uv had a purpose somewhere. He's smoking evil out into the open. No telling what all they'd be if I had the pair of those spy glasses my late husband used to dangle wherever we went. But the pawn got em now, now you know. . . ."

"Mrs. Quick, shut up," a voice cried.

The fireman stopped aiming at the steeple with water. Soon all the hoses were laid in a tangle on the ground. The fire engines started up the street and stopped at a distance. The lights with the murder-red and white were trained like spotlight cannon on the steeple. As the steeple began to sway dizzy, the people on the hill walked backwards, at first slowly and then faster, fleeing to the open space behind the lookout. There wasn't a rush and tangle but a steady, scared moving away. Coin went with them, his heart like a glass fit to break.

Everybody stopped. There was a falling Niagara Falls roar from the crowd that rose up and died down again as a first crack in the middle of the steeple spread down, zigzagging like a lightning snake lower and lower. The clock burst out and flew, winding parts zinged in the air and the four flat faces skipped, leveled, and settled. Then, one

23

by one, the bricks began to speed everywhere in twos and threes and fifteens, shot from a bean-shooter machine. The flames waved out like battle flags. Pitchforks of fire. Hard, red birds fighting in the sky, in smoke and stink. Lances of steel.

It was exactly midnight. Coin heard the first bell from the churches of Brooklyn strike the hour. Every night they struck the midnight hour. The moaning crowd became gradually silent. The bells from Nazarene, Siloam, St. Anthony's, the Baptist Temple, Green Avenue Presbyterian, the Church of the Ascension, St. Anne's, Claremont Congregational, Concord Baptist ... mostly they came in unison, sometimes a note apart, crossing each other. All the notes were there. Bong four. Alto, soprano, bass. The Lafayette Church of Christ was the deepest and longest and swelled between the others, holding them together like the organ of the Corinthian Baptist Church used to hold the whole choir. Bong six. Those golden pipes were folding in the heat at this minute, Coin saw. Bong nine. They bowed to right and left, sometimes backwards or to each other in their heat, and collapsed with the gold peeling, fluttering down like broken butterflies. Bong twelve. A little ringing was left in the air. Then it stopped altogether.

The funeral for his church was over.

Coin couldn't wipe the tears away from his eyes fast enough to dry his face before Miss Horwitz came, followed by his father.

"Well, Mr. Foreman," Miss Horwitz smiled at

the wreck below, "it looks like God has at last let you down."

Mr. Foreman put his arm about Coin's shoulder gently. It was a welcome. His father's hair was so gray now. His father's voice was soft, soft like when you can't talk loud after waking up when a dream has been bad.

"Miss Horwitz, I don't know how you pray, I don't know when. I don't care. But for me and my children ... our ... our lives were spent in that church, my children were baptized in that pool, my wife was buried from there. And to all these people there was something between those walls that made life bearable. We knew we could never be alone because God was in there with us. Laugh to yourself, make fun alone, but don't laugh at our disaster. Don't laugh at our faith before the children. We will build again. Good night."

Something burst and lit up the park for a second, but in that time Coin thought he saw something like thorns for Jesus in Miss Horwitz's eyes.

His father walked slowly down the hill feeling his way. Coin knew that there would be no scoldings from him. Somehow he didn't care one way or the other about punishments. Punishments passed just as lights went out and would go on once more. His father took the long way round the hill as if he didn't want to speak to the others. Coin was glad for that and for the arm on his shoulder. If he had known how to say it he would have repented something or the other to his father. He didn't know how to say or do anything. He hadn't even been able to reach Kentucky when he was on the train for it. He had failed somehow. The search for his friend Ferris had ended in this fire. He couldn't speak to his father who loved him so much and say that he'd take a paper route and save all the money to help "rebuild again." He felt lost and terrified, like sleeping in a room where there was a dead rat in the wall you couldn't locate but you had to sleep there just the same. There was no other place to lay your head.

Going home now down the winding Fort Green Park Road. Going home now with his father's tired hand on his tired shoulder. Going home to a slap from Agnes and giggles from Woody and Bernice.

He would have another birthday soon after this summer. Sometimes it came Thanksgiving Day or the day before or the day after. They would say, as always, with juicy smiles, "Thanksgiving dinner is your birthday dinner. There isn't a boy alive who has such a dinner on his birthday." Even if he had never been born they would have had Thanksgiving dinner.

Fireflies lit the bushes as he and his father passed. Such little fires, but they were safe and glowed and couldn't burn a gnat.

"They're pretty," said Mr. Foreman.

"They sure are," answered Coin.

He wished he could go to sleep and wake up on another birthday when he was old enough to march into the world and erase everything that wasn't a wonder. But now he was without teachers or a chalk to mark his globe. Of course he had gone and had been brought back by the police. But ten years was better than nine years old. At least he had learned about the deaf and dumb and blind. He had expected to come back with new aggies and diamonds for Esther and the golden synagogue chair for his father to sit in. He had come back to Revelation in the Bible instead. The end of that book was only the beginning for him. As he listened to nothing in the silent darkness he heard the deaf and dumb people from the train signal language to him in semaphore. They had been locked in dark closets and had found a way out. Now he had to sleep before tomorrow. He would figure out why the church burned down and why God worked in mysterious ways and not in the open. But no matter what answers he found, there would always be the burned bones of Deaconess Westerfield's hump, the thorns for Jesus in Miss Horwitz's eyes.

Chapter Two

Since Coin had been away, his brother Woody had become a collector, but Coin couldn't find out what he was collecting or where whatever it was was stored. He had looked high and low in the house for clues. Chris O'Connor and Abie Fox were in on the secret but they walked around mysterious as if they didn't understand what Coin was talking about. Almost every weekend or holiday the kids disappeared from the block, following Woody. It was impossible for Coin to follow them because they tricked him and all the others who weren't in their gang by going in different directions. You couldn't follow all of them at once. Coin decided to wait and see; he knew that if the collecting secret were really something, Woody would have to tell him sometime instead of saying that he was too young to know, and even if he was too young he just might tell on them and then there *would* be hell to pay. Deciding that they were doing something dirty or bad, Coin would wait. He had begun to grow hairs in important places and that would give him Samson strength!

One evening when he and his father were alone together in the backyard, Mr. Foreman asked Coin what he had done in school that day.

"Nothing much, Popa."

"You must have done something. Didn't anything happen?"

"Well, William said he was going to kill me."

His father looked up from his weeding. "Who's William?"

"One of the boys at school."

"I see."

"He's bigger than I am and he carries a long whip in his back pocket."

"I'll go up one of these days and see your teacher. Maybe we can get you transferred to another school."

"No. There are Williams in every school," Coin answered, tracing designs in the dirt. He had to say something.

Mr. Foreman took out one of his large handkerchiefs and coughed into it, wiped his nose, and looked at him quietly for a long time. Coin kept tracing his designs until his father went into the house.

Two days later his father brought him a large white humpy seashell with pink lining and sea tracings about the edges. Coin thanked him and went into the backyard and sat on a box under the grape arbor. He put the shell to one ear and began to listen. There was a low murmur, a call from faraway, a magic sound, steady but back and forth. Voices in the sea and one word over and over from his geography book: Mesopotamia, Mesopotamia, Mesopotamia. The voice of a beckoning finger. Mesopotamia. Sometimes there were other words, too, but that one word was always there calling him away from the house; his father's cough, Woody's dirty words, Esther's smile, Miss Horwitz's detective eyes. He would sit for hours dreaming, shifting the shell from ear to ear. He might be a sailor one day and see the high and low of things. This was better than Woody's collecting secret, this was all his own. His sailor-boy dreams shipped him over the world. He might be Captain Coin Foreman someday, barking out orders near Mesopotamia.

Three weeks before Thanksgiving when Coin was running an errand for Agnes, he found out what Woody had been doing. Coming home from New Lots, on the edge of the woods, he noticed the twilight sun hit metal between trees and clumps of wornout bushes. That didn't attract his attention so much as a knocking on the metal, then a voice from inside, and an answer from without. It sounded like Woody and Chris O'Connor from the laughter inside. Creeping up close, he hid himself behind bushes to watch and listen. Sure enough there came Abie Schneider looking right and left like a hunter.

He stopped at the door and gave a complicated knock. Woody's voice answered loud from within.

"The Open Kimono."

Abie scratched his head. Coin was bewildered.

"Aw, it's not fair, I can't think of nothing," cried Abie.

Woody's voice came back, "You'd better think of something or you don't get in."

"OK, Woody, OK, you'll be sorry. I can't think of nothing."

"You're a big dope, Abie." That must be Chris O'Connor's voice.

"If you don't add to the collection, remember, out you go."

"I got it now," laughed Abie.

"Say it!"

Abie shouted, "By Seymore Hare." The door was opened to gangs of laughter.

When Teddie Estabrook marched up to the door, there was the same rrap, rrap, bing, bing, rrap.

Woody's voice sang out, "I Go Often."

"By Lucy Bowels!"

The shouts went up again as Teddie barged in.

Coin wondered what he could think up to get in. But you didn't think up anything, Woody did that. You had to make the answers. He edged up to the window that had broken bottles along the ledge and peeked in carefully. There they were all seated around egg crates made like a table, playing the Ouija Board. On the walls were the printed signs. *I Go Often* by Lucy Bowels, *The Yellow Stream* by

I. P. Standing, *A Spot on the Wall* by Whoo Flung Dung, *The Purple Balls* by Won Hung Lowe, *The Driving Rod* by Dick Peters, *The Open Kimono* by Ophelia Toitt, and so forth and so forth, all around the room. There was a candle in one corner of the table that sent shadows to the walls against the coming dark. He had known it was something dirty, and his brother Oscar must have taught them that game. Shucks, he didn't care. Ha, ha, if he ever told them about Uncle Troy and Mrs. Walker and what he had seen and knew about from Washington, D.C., they'd be surprised. Ha, ha. He wasn't going to get mixed up in any of that stuff. Just the same, on the way back home he couldn't get his mind off titles and wondered what Ferris would have thought up. Probably something like *I Wake Up Early* by Ann Will Hardin!

"Congratulations, daught, it seems like old times again to have the family together. Well almost . . . except for your brother Oscar. I hope that reform school reforms him proper."

"I ain't seen him since he was with the Edwards girl. . . ."

"Bernice, not ain't, haven't," interrupted Agnes.

"Well, haven't . . . I haven't seen him since he was with the Edwards girl at the church fair two weeks ago."

"Well, I hope we can prevail upon the school to let him loose for Christmas. It would be first rate to have you all under the same roof, yessirre-Bob, it would."

Coin noticed that Agnes kept her lips squeezed together while his father spoke. Everytime his father was smiley, like tonight, Agnes seemed to have some ace of spades or other in the back of her mind.

"Popa," she said, "speaking of roofs ... don't you think it would be nice if we moved to another place ... a better neighborhood? The children are growing up now and soon Bernice will be wanting to bring her friends around. She's fifteen and it would be better for her to meet her boyfriends. ..."

Woody mumbled, "She hasn't got no boyfriends, let alone friends," and giggled.

"I have a right to have a boyfriend like everybody else, so there," answered Bernice.

Coin struck his brother's knee with his knee under the table. Woody let go a big "Ouch."

"What in the world is going on here?" Mr. Foreman said. "Whatever it is stop this minute. All three of you."

Agnes continued. "I've seen several places, and Miss Horwitz says that. ..."

"Agnes, I have told you time and time again not to mention that woman's name to me, or in my house."

"Or in *your* house." Agnes's voice seemed to crack Mr. Foreman's knuckles. Coin wanted to say excuse me but there was no chance. He sat there wishing for his shell to carry him away from all the bickering he had heard a trillion times since Mama died.

"Sorry, Popa, I just thought it would be good to have more room. The boys are getting older and should have a room to themselves."

"I understand all that, Agnes. You're a new generation and should keep up-to-date. I've just gotten used to being here."

"We could move nearer the church." It looked like Agnes was trying to stuff candy down Popa's throat.

"There is no church."

"Well, when they build again."

Popa looked over all their heads, looking at some other person in the room. "Daught, try to make yourself and the children comfortable here for a while longer. I doubt if it will be too long."

"All right, Popa, if that is what you want."

"That is what I wish."

"Bernice, help me serve up the food." Agnes and Bernice went into the kitchen. Popa was still looking faraway.

Agnes returned presently with the roast, followed by Bernice carrying a platter of baked potatoes, corn, and peas. Mr. Foreman heaped the plates in silence. Since their mother died, Agnes was trying out the new method on all of them. Nearly everything about the family was discussed even with the children around. "It will give them a sense of responsibility. They should know all the problems we face and will be able to understand why we do what we do."

Now Agnes was talking again in the quiet voice that had trouble at the bottom of it.

"I won't bring this up again, Popa, but I don't think it's Christian not to let Lucy come to the house ... please let me finish ... everything you say about Lucy is right in a way. She is bitter and angry with the whole world when you watch her just so. But underneath she's not that way at all. I'm not saying that she's been hurt and that's why she acts the way she does. We know that. (We, Coin thought, don't know nothing.) It's worse than that; nothing has ever happened to Lucy. Nothing human. She's almost fifty and alone—perhaps more than fifty. Alone inside. I think she considers us her family. Mama was kind. She spread her love and consideration to anyone who needed it and Lucy was included, just as Mrs. Carth was and all Berriman Street. Lucy feels that I'm her sister. She needs the children to belong. If she's sometimes been disrespectful to you, I think it's only loneliness, wishing she was the head of a family, hoping to create something."

Mr. Foreman carefully cut his piece of roast before he answered. "Why, daught, you're quite a philosopher. Let her come if she feels that way. What you say is probably true. No matter how she got the way she is, she is that way. You've got too much of your mother in you to turn her out. Maybe you can change her. I hope so because she's a thorn in my

36

side. I know she's been working since she was no older than Coin. Well, daught, what she's been through the whole race has been through. I'm asking you to watch out. The woman doesn't even laugh except *at* somebody. She's got what my mother used to call bile for blood."

"You don't understand, Popa. Please pass the vegetables to Bernice." The matter was settled for now and they ate in silence, chewing hard to get all the strength out of the food and to keep from looking at each other.

In the midst of dessert Agnes broke the silence. "For days no one has talked of anything else hardly except the Corinthian Baptist Church Rally in Madison Square Garden." She looked at her father knowing he would be pleased to talk about the church instead of Miss Horwitz.

"Why, daught," his father said to Agnes, "this will be the biggest demonstration of faith in the church that this city has seen. The mayor will be there and delegates from all the churches in Brooklyn. We ought to raise enough money to build three edifices."

"Yes, I know, Popa. But how's your speech?"

"Why, daught, I've written and rewritten my speech until it's blue in the face." Mr. Foreman gave a satisfied laugh.

"It's not too long, Popa?"

"I think it will suffice."

"Just so it's not too long." Agnes gave him a kiss and squeezed his arm. Even *she* was proud that his father would be delivering a message in Madison Square Garden, Manhattan, where the circus was held each year.

While Coin was dressing up just before the rally, Woody came in. "Do you know what, Coin, you oughtta see Miss Lucy. She's dressed to kill. She's put on her rabbit fur and her cat fur and her rat fur, *and* a hat with chicken feathers sticking out of it; she's got on paint and powder. Looks like undertaker's makeup to me, she's that stingy. Well, I'm not gonna sit next to her and have the whole Madison Square Garden staring. Boy, that fur smells like it ain't been cured." They nudged one another and performed some light wrestling because Miss Horwitz would be the clown of the rally.

"I sure wish I had a camera. I'd take her picture front, back, sideways, upside down, and sell them for souvenirs. They'd sell like hot dogs. When she came in the door just now, Popa had to turn his face to the wall to keep from laughing in her face. Then he said good evening and orated on how she was dressed up. She threw that rabbit fur about her neck and told him thank you with a giggle and went to Agnes's room for more compliments, probably."

Finally they were all gathered into the limousine the church had sent for Popa. "Well," said Mr. Foreman, "it's nice for all of us to be under one roof again and traveling in style. All except Oscar, my namesake. I wonder . . . Agnes, have you

38

heard from the school upstate, how he's getting along? I hope we can have him down for Christmas, so we can celebrate properly."

"We haven't heard a word from him for a long time. Maybe it's best, Popa, for him to just stay there until his conduct discharge comes through."

"You might be right, daught. But Momps would want us all to be together, especially at Christmas."

"She's exactly right," Miss Horwitz shot between her teeth. Coin began to fidget.

"Anything wrong, son?" Mr. Foreman said.

"Nothing, Popa, only my pants are tight," Coin answered. His pants were OK, he didn't want to witness an open fight. So he slid into a lie.

"Mr. Courtland promised me a suit for each of you boys. They might be here for Christmas and then you and Woody can dress up as classy as Miss Horwitz here."

"Popa!" muttered Agnes.

"Don't worry about me, Agnes," tossed Miss Horwitz. Coin hoped that her rabbit fur wouldn't get on his dark suit.

Bernice stirred. "Popa, how big is Madison Square Garden?"

"As big as *we've* got in New York."

"And you're speaking there tonight?"

"Yes, Bernice."

"Mmm ... mmm ... mmm," Bernice replied. She was putting Miss Horwitz smack in her place. Her father was something; so there! Coin glanced at his father in his cutaway suit. He looked just as fine as a picture, and his hedge mustache was cut to perfection. He was really fixed up.

Outside the Garden was a band that played as their limousine drove up. Popa brightened and sat up straight. They all sat up too. Even Miss Horwitz, adjusting her furs that let out sudden animal smells. She pretended to be part of the welcome. Welcome, Miss Lucy Bowels, welcome! Mr. Foreman got out first and gave his hand to Agnes, Bernice, and finally to Miss Horwitz. He wouldn't let the driver do it. Woody and Coin scrambled out as best they could. They all walked in together. Mr. Foreman saw them seated in the front row and then left for the platform, rattling the papers for his speech as he ascended the rostrum. Coin watched his father greet Reverend Brooks and the other deacons and finally the mayor. He glanced out of the corner of his eye at Miss Horwitz. She was huffy in her furs, pretending not to notice what was taking place. Coin thought: she'd better not get so high, when the people come milling into her those furs will smother them in animal-stinking sweat.

It wasn't like a circus at all. But banners to Christ were so bright they burst into his eyes. They were everywhere. They seemed umpteen-feet tall and wide. They ranged around the Garden. *We Will Rebuild Again; Christ Is Our General; Hallelujah: We Return; We Cometh Again to Fix a New Jerusalem; Thy Wages Are Not for Sin, But for Our Lord; Doubt Not That You Will Die; Collect*

40

Virtue: Those Who Do Not Will Perish; Give for His Kingdom on Earth or You Will Not Be Blessed and whatnot all about.

Coin would have been frightened but his father was on the stage, quiet and ready to consider the propositions of all banners, all hoping, all death by fire, air, rail, or natural. No darkness would ever cover them. His father presided in Madison Square Garden. Besides Coin had taken his paper route, had given most of the change he got to rebuild the church. Woody said he was a fool; Miss Horwitz, when she heard about it, asked him if the Lord was going to send him to college when the time came; Agnes suggested that he give some to the church fund and save some for his future; Popa told him to do what was in his heart; Bernice told him that what he gave would buy about fifty bricks and she left it at that; Mrs. Quick got wind of his project and told him to pray on it for an answer. Pray for his mother's sake. When the people in the neighborhood heard what Coin was doing, they gave him tips and told their friends to buy their papers from him. Mrs. Fox and Mrs. Jeffers and the Richardsons helped a lot. And so he had the courage to do what his mother would have wanted him to do. His marks in school were better than average. Ha, ha. Let Miss Horwitz and the rest put that in their pipes and smoke it.

Through announcements in the papers and the churches of Brooklyn, it had been suggested that the women attending the rally wear white for the occasion. (Miss Horwitz and Agnes ignored the suggestion.) The place was filling up and soon all the banks of balconies and the main floor were crowded. There were more white dresses than anything else. Mr. Foreman arose and rapped his gavel until silence came. He announced that they were about to begin, that the arena was crowded with those who had felt it in their hearts to help rebuild an edifice to the Lord where they could worship again, to be called the *New* Corinthian Baptist Church, and he continued, reading from the Bible: "For as Paul has written: 'Unto the church of God which is at Corinth, to them that are sanctified in Christ Jesus, called to be saints. . . . Grace be unto you, and peace, from God our Father, and *from* the Lord Jesus Christ.' Now this message has been handed down to us from generation to generation. It is only right and fitting that one of God's men, Reverend Brooks, pastor of the Corinthian Baptist Church, be called upon to preside over this vast congregation and lead us in gracious prayer." Mr. Foreman sat down, tossing up the tails of his cutaway so as not to wrinkle them.

Reverend Brooks's prayer was short and crisp. At the end he requested the entire gathering to sing "Give All Thy Hath to the Lord."

Miss Horwitz, in a loud whisper, said, "He's smart, he's going to make them ask for the money themselves from themselves. That's a new twist. And I suppose it will work."

Thousands arose and sang. They swayed to the

tune, batting their bodies to the tennis-match rhythm of the song.

The program was long and the arena got hotter and hotter. Neither did Miss Horwitz take off her furs that were smelling. They were foul in the air and made what Mrs. Quick had once called asthma in the nose.

After the collection had been taken, Mr. Foreman got up to make the speech he had composed. The organ had been shut off. Silence was the order of his father's hour. Mr. Foreman looked over the balconies first and then to down below. Coin thought once that he gazed at him.

"Children of our God," he pronounced, "I have been asked to say a few words while the financial counting is being made. We gathered here to rebuild another church, dedicated to our God and His Son. All of you who have contributed, please stand. Thank you for the Lord and His Son Who abideth among us." He waited for a moment.

The whole arena was standing in a body. Except Miss Horwitz. Except Miss Horwitz. Nobody noticed the shame but Coin. Each eye, including Agnes's and Bernice's and Woody's, was pinned on the rostrum from where his father spoke. And he concluded in *less* than due time: "Whatever has been taken up, or pledged, will be put down for all of us to enjoy in God's name in our new home. Even children have felt the need to cast forward their earnings. In this place where we are causing the new resurrection of our church, I want you to think on the future, not the past. Whatever lit the fire in our church, do not be dismayed, the Lord will seek the reason out. Evil will not conquer but when you see the inkling of its root, act! Now let all in this company rise again and march toward Zion."

White handkerchiefs waved in the air. The organ struck up "We're Marching to Zion." Mr. Foreman took out his white handkerchief and waved with them. Then he sat down with satisfaction, panting hard. "We're marching to Zion, beautiful, beautiful Zion. . . ."

"That was short," commented Agnes.

"And sweet," replied Bernice.

"Humph," was all Miss Horwitz sounded.

He said the *children* had cast forth their earnings, thought Coin. That meant *him*. He had been mentioned before thousands even if they didn't know him. But Agnes knew and Miss Horwitz and Bernice and Woody and Mrs. Quick *and* the Lord. But none of them said a word.

The service was over and the people marched out, orderly, row by row, singing the hymn, "We're Marching to Zion." But his father stayed on the platform silent and alone, his head was hung forward. Mrs. Quick said, "Deacon Foreman don't seem so well." She hustled up her bag and walked quickly to the rostrum. The family followed.

We're marching to Zion,
Beautiful, beautiful Zion. . . .

The audience was still marching out to Zion in black and white order. On the rostrum Mr. Foreman sat in his chair, grasping the arms, counting out the rhythm, panting. To Coin he seemed in a trance as they gathered about. Mrs. Quick shot forward, saying to Agnes, "Do you reckon a little brandy will help him out?" Mr. Foreman had stopped his rhythm and his head was at the back of the chair. He was breathing hard.

Agnes's voice had alarm in it. "There's no brandy around, Mrs. Quick. This is a church rally."

"Well now," replied Mrs. Quick, "I think I've got a drop or two right here in my purse. We have to be prepared at all times for all emergencies." And she snapped her purse open and produced a medicine bottle of brandy and held it to Mr. Foreman's lips.

"There now," she giggled, "let's see what happens." And sure enough his father came to. In a few minutes he was strong enough for them to help him to the limousine. Miss Horwitz had yet to say a word. She held her lips in a slippery smile.

It wasn't that his father was sick, the doctor said. He was pining away, wasting away. "Miss Foreman, I don't know what else to say." Then he left with a sigh. Coin heard the words plain from the front room.

Time after time he had watched his father sitting in the backyard, gazing at the last of the vegetables he had grown. Coin would go out in the late afternoon with blankets for his shoulders and his knees. He wrapped his father against the cold. Mr. Foreman said, as always, "Thank you." And that was all. Near night Coin and Woody helped him to the dining room for his dinner and afterwards to bed. He never said much except "thank you."

One night Coin woke up and his father was talking in his sleep. The only word he understood was "Naomi." His mother's name. The next day the weather began to get real cold.

His father didn't go out after that. He only read his Bible and was not concerned when Agnes brought broth. Sometimes he asked her to leave it there and read to him. Sometimes he drank it or ate a bit of solid food Agnes had prepared special, or went to the bathroom and stayed a long time. Mostly, Coin sensed, he was waiting for something to fold him away. The autumn went by, day after day, the leaves broke away from the trees. Bernice and Woody tiptoed around after school and Coin did too.

The last day of November Miss Lucy Horwitz visited with her black self! But Popa, thank goodness, didn't notice. She went directly to Agnes's room. Coin and Woody were playing a game of cards with Bernice looking on. They played in silence. Presently Agnes appeared in the doorway. She inspected the game. She inspected them.

"Why don't you put those cards up?" she said softly.

"Must we, Agnes?" Bernice said in her usual popcorn voice.

"Yes, yes, I think so," Agnes replied. She was snapping her fingernails. Bernice asked why. Agnes proceeded to the table and took up the cards one by one until she had the pack in her hands. She slipped the deck neatly into its case. Coin saw Miss Horwitz standing in the doorway. There were shadows around her smile.

"I don't know now, I've sent for the doctor, but I think your father is dead." Coin had passed by his father just a little time before and thought he was sleeping.

What Coin felt now was different by yards from when his mother was ill and close to dying. He had expected that his mother could never die because of God and the love of her friends and family and the administrations of Mrs. Quick, because of the countless prayers and medicines and orange juice, because of his communion for her and her strength at the head of the dinner table each and every night. He felt she couldn't die because Popa needed her, and she had loved him and almost everybody. Even the mean ones, like Miss Lucy and Mrs. Carth who hated everybody, loved Mama. Now with Popa it was different. He had been away all day at work, and at night it was meetings or the garden. He was the one who had to use the strap and call your attention to the bad things done. He read the Bible to you and argued the Bible pronouncements of his favorite prophets. He asked you to sit on a stack of books once a month and he cut your hair: cut, cut, cut, slowly, for what seemed like hours.

When he began to just sit around, not talking, not reading, only looking and nodding, his hair got almost completely dandelion white and thin in October and November. His friends came and sat with him and he made some effort to talk, but not much. Mr. Courtland, his boss, rode all the way from Manhattan in a taxi; the deacons and deaconesses came and prayed. The doctor arrived and examined and left, saying there was nothing he could find wrong. His father was pining away from a broken heart. Coin had sensed then that the fountain of his father's days was drying up. And so the news of his father's death had been prepared for. Even the weather seemed to be in cahoots with death. Late, late in cold November, right after Coin's birthday, the leaves were dying or dead, some leftover chrysanthemums in the backyard held on, sudden sunsets and darkness, leaves burning along the gutters, all this said winter and death to Coin. Overcoats and rubbers again. And then on his birthday his father came to the table so as not to miss his thirteenth birthday. He sat in his great gray robe. As Coin blew out the candles, Popa made a joke:

"Birthday cakes are unsanitary. All the breath and spittle blowing out the candles of your years."

After that he had done a strange thing. He took out his big, golden watch and handed it to Agnes, looking at Coin.

"Give it to Coin when he's old enough to wear it. Every once in a while until then, let him hold it against his ear." They all looked at Coin. He wanted to go to the bathroom or drink some water. Then Popa got up, saying he was going to retire for the night. He walked to the bathroom, turned and said, "Happy birthday, son." Agnes looked at Coin. "Would you like to keep it overnight, Coin?" she said.

"No," he had said, "I'll listen to it tomorrow." His birthday was over. He saw the picture of himself like he was a little while ago, blowing out "the candles of his years," and his father in the light of a last supper.

After the doctor left, stretching his hand out in sympathy to all of them including Miss Horwitz, Bernice and Woody went quietly down the steps; Coin lay down on his bed; Agnes and Miss Horwitz, talking across the table in belly whispers, waited for Undertaker Ward. Coin heard a knock at the door. It was Mrs. Renaldo.

"Is it finished?" she asked. Her voice had Chianti wine in it and graveyard crosses.

"It is finished," answered Agnes. Her sigh ended the season. Winter had truly begun. Then he heard the door close and in a while, overheard, Mrs. Renaldo was walking with her dead across her floor.

"Lucy," Agnes was talking, "two days ago when Popa was sitting by the window, he asked me to play 'To a Wild Rose' by MacDowell. And I said,

'Popa, I didn't know you liked that kind of music.' Guess what he said? 'You never inquired, daught.' He was right. I never did inquire. I never noticed that his hair had grown so white until Coin's birthday, when he handed me the watch. I guess I was thinking about Harry most of the time. And now Harry's married and I have a bunch of kids on my hands. Since Mama died, I've let the children go to seed, running after Harry. Harry's left. I don't know how I'll manage, but I'll manage. If Harry were here to help, it would be different. But Harry's not here and Popa's dead." Agnes seemed to squeeze tears into his bed.

"I'll help you, Agnes."

"Thank you, Lucy. You know what? Let's make this the biggest Christmas for the children."

The biggest Christmas of all. He'd had the biggest after his mother died, when his father attempted the biggest Christmas of all. That was the holiday! After the breakfast of eggs, sausage, cereal, fruit juice, biscuits, milk, coffee, and whatnot, Agnes read a story from Hans Christian Andersen about the little match girl who had sold no matches all day. Her feet were cold, her mouth was cold, she was ice cold. She began to light her matches to keep warm; at each light she saw something wonderful. Presently her grandmother, who had been dead, appeared and beckoned her. She went. Later they found the little girl dead with a smile on her face in a doorway. It was Christmas morning; for them so-sad stories were fairy tales, anyway, and didn't matter. In a little while, the glory of their presents would come. At the end of the story, Popa read the real Christmas story from the Bible. He even made the straw in the manger Christian and mysterious. The wise men really juggled jewels before Jesus. They had taken the stars from the sky, Coin thought, and made them shine before the newborn king. Oh, Popa read of bright hallelujahs. Everybody enjoyed it, too. At last they all marched to the door of the front room. The key was turned and then taken out. Popa kept the suspense going. He stood there happy as a lark eating sunlight.

"Agnes, do you suppose these children have had enough to eat?"

Agnes was all for going in now. There was the tree, as he opened the door. It was the lamp of the world, plucked from fairyland. Agnes was smiling. They saw the star on top and inspected the bright balls of green and silver, red, blue; there was every holiday color on the tree, sparkling. "The parables of the world are blessed there," his father announced in his special voice, "I want you all to range around me with your eyes closed and your minds set on your Christmas wish." They gathered around. "Let us all sing: 'Praise God from Whom All Blessings Flow.' "

They sang out loud. When they finished, Popa told them to open their eyes. The tree still shone there. They were ready to grab for their presents. Only the cut-down suits Mr. Courtland had sent for Woody and Coin were under the tree, folded: his boys' cut-down suits, dead dummies of cloth: second-hand.

Three days later the inspector from the reform school called to tell them that Oscar had been caught with a laundry bag of presents over his shoulder. Maybe he was going to pawn them for his girl friends or something. Coin did not know. When he and Woody had tried on the cut-down suits from Mr. Courtland, they didn't fit, anyway. The Christmas of all!

After his father died he made himself scarce. He found a book called *Pilgrim's Progress*, decided to read it while the processions of neighbors and church folk paraded in and out like they owned death and his father. No sooner had he opened the book but he found a letter. He was sitting in the backyard, wrapped up in blankets, ready to die like Popa, away from it all. Here it was, dated 1896. Lord have good mercy! His mother and father were dead in their death; so he read it:

112 Myrtle Ave.
Brooklyn, N.Y.
Feb. 13, 1896

My Dear Naomi:

Your dear letter bearing its ripe fruit of thought came in the 10 o'clock mail on Wednesday. I was busy waiting on a customer in my store and afterwards came the postman. I immediately grew anxious as well as expectant; I was not disappointed, for at a mere glance I saw that it was from you.

Your promptness is love and your expressions charm. I was very much animated by your wit in reference to the storm and my being blown away. I wonder does the same apply to my friend? (Laughter)

The poet Saxe says, "To be a good woman is better than to be a fine lady," and "The proper study of mankind is man, but the most perplexing one no doubt is woman." (Laughter)

I am glad to write you that I am very well and all seems to be going well. We are now getting our material together for the children to collect for Easter, It is my desire to make a large contribution to the church, I am going to ask the Lord for $150—one hundred and fifty dollars. Now will you remember me in your prayers that liberal hearts may encourage the children in this worthy effort.

The Lord has sent showers of blessings upon us on Monday night—in the meeting we had about fifteen mourners and two converts and, as you so aptly wished, we are having a delightful period in the vineyard of the Lord.

I want to ask you to think over the subject of coming to visit your cousin in Newark during the coming summer. If you will come, then I shall make a proposition to you whereby relieving you of all the expense that would tend to hinder you from doing so.

'You know I want to see you very bad and as it is perhaps easy for you to comply with this request, I hope you will give it your most careful consideration.

I live for those who love us, whose hearts are kind and true, for the heaven that smiles above me and awaits my spirit too.

God be with you always. Amen.

Yours sincerely and faithfully,
Oscar

Coin put the letter down, keeping one hand over it. He did not feel like crying. His father and mother were close again at last. He had the written truth, under his hand, of the beginning of their trials and tribulations which had ended three hours ago. He thought it might be good for him to keep this letter and ponder it and read in *Pilgrim's Progress* what they had read, perhaps together, at 112 Myrtle Avenue. He held his parents' treasures for a moment, laid them on the chair, then folded the blankets that had covered Popa over his arm and went upstairs, not crying, but afraid.

Three days later they buried Popa. He was borne like easy, inconvenient plunder to the grave. Agnes and Miss Horwitz were all in black for the day. Woody, Bernice and Coin followed; after them, the deacons and deaconesses, led by the pastor. Mr. Foreman was lowered to his final home.

Chapter Three

One night about six o'clock, after dinner, Agnes asked Woody and Bernice and Coin to stay in for a while, she wanted to have a family conference with all of them present. Coin knew something was askew when Miss Horwitz came through the dining room looking like she had swallowed at least a dozen jokes. She smiled at all of them, showing her raisin teeth, and saying that after they had talked with Agnes she had a treat for them. Then she left, swallowing more jokes. The children looked at each other and then back at Agnes. Bernice looked wise and black and sad.

"Why don't we all sit around the table," Agnes commanded, as if she were in her classroom. When they were all seated she began. "You know that I've always wanted to own a house, get out of this run-down neighborhood to where we all could have friends that come up to the standards your mother and father tried to set for us. Well, it looks like my dream and theirs for all of us is coming true."

Coin watched the pout on Bernice's mouth become her whole face. He had never seen Woody so quiet as when he asked, "You mean I gotta . . . ?"

"Have to," corrected Agnes.

" . . . gotta leave Chris and Abie and the gang?" Woody was close to tears.

Bernice ripped into what Agnes had said. "Listen, Agnes. . . ." Her voice made the air around Coin bleed.

"Watch your tone, young lady. . . ."

" . . . I don't want to be no lady, I want to be a woman like Mama and Mrs. Jeffers and Mrs. Fox. You mean to say they're not good enough for us and we can't play with their children because they're poor? They all go to church or the synagogue. Don't come telling me about no standards. And Aunt Harriet was coming to live with us right after Popa died; even her trunks arrived. A week ago the Railway Express took them back. I bet you thought Mama's sister wasn't good enough! And besides. . . ." She began to cry so hard the tears seemed to pop out, hitting them all. Agnes's mouth became a hard, sucked-in line, holding her temper straight, but Bernice continued like floods couldn't drown her out.

"Listen, Agnes, please for once listen. I know you're older than us and have to put up with us because you promised Mama and Popa to take care of us until we're grown ... and you do love us ... but do we have to put up with *her*?"

"*Her*," repeated Agnes, so calm she seemed to be threading needles.

"Yes, you know as well as me who her is, *Miss Lucy*, that's who."

It was crazy. All Coin could think of was that dirty rhyme he'd learned in the streets. It went through his head so fast and nasty tears came to his eyes and he wanted to laugh:

I went downtown to see Miss Lucy,
Gave her two cents to see her pussy,
Pussy so black,
I couldn't see the crack.
I asked Miss Lucy
For my two cents back.

"I never mentioned Miss Horwitz," Agnes said. "Did either of you boys hear me mention her this evening?" Woody and Coin wouldn't open their mouths.

"Of course they didn't," continued Bernice, "because *you didn't* mention her name; you didn't mean to mention it. And she coming through here promising us some kind of treat or other. If it's ice cream I bet she's spit in it, she's that shitty. . . ."

Agnes slapped first one of Bernice's cheeks and then the other. Bernice just went on. ". . . and Popa didn't like her. He said it before all of us. Miss Horwitz is buying the house with you or you're buying it with her, it doesn't matter which. And if you ever slap me again when I'm telling the truth, you'll hear from me even if you fly to Timbuktu." Then Bernice sat down again at the table and cried black tears. Agnes went over and put her arms about her. "I'm sorry, Bernice, I'm sorry, I'm doing the best I know how." Bernice shook her off and through her weeping said, "You ain't sorry. My Mama's dead."

Those were the last words he heard Bernice utter around the house for two weeks. She would stay in the backyard beneath the grape arbor with her blackboard, hour after hour, drawing pictures of all sorts of things. Then she'd erase them. Once Coin thought he saw a great big heart in red chalk with the regular arrow through it and initials he couldn't make out. She was beside herself. Esther told him later that she ate only the Jewish candy, halvah. Each night Bernice crept home.

Once, when the truant officer saw her on the street, Esther told that Bernice said, "I'll go away, wherever you say." But the officer left. So Coin decided to speak to her. There was nothing else to do. Two days later after school he found her sitting on the steps of the dark hall that led to their apartment. As he walked toward her she let down her head and wept little tears, tired and old. She reminded him of Mrs. Renaldo waiting for the resurrection of her dead. He thought of the song "Blessed Be the Tie That Binds," that they always sang in church. He decided to whistle it, softly, to ignore her and draw her attention, too. The words were in him, though, as he whistled underneath his breath: "Blessed be the tie that binds our hearts in Christian love, the fellowship. . . ." Bernice looked up and Woody, who must have entered on sneakers, joined in with a broken voice. And so the three of them sang there against the enemy. They were children and had to do what their elders said had to be done. Softly they finished the song in a ragged way. There was no talk as they walked up the stairs where their lives had been lived. They had to do Agnes's and Miss Horwitz's will because they did not have another plan.

The main one he wanted to say good-bye to was Esther. Not that he wouldn't see her anymore. This was the end of Berriman Street for him. He *had* wandered around, seen a few states. He was in Brownsville Junior High, would enter junior high somewhere else. And as Agnes said, it would be better. She was a teacher and she should know. He settled into the grape arbor where he had gone when his mother died, where he had buried his best cat, where Bernice had painted pictures of faces of boys and a heart with initials he couldn't make out; this was a place fifty feet from where his mother had tossed a paper rose to his father. He would sit here till he died.

All Esther had to do was open the cellar steps from the outside and get through the cellar to the backyard. It was easier than skipping rope. As he waited a twilight came down, only a little paler than the communion juice he drank on Sundays.

There was a breeze. His Popa had worked this garden. The windows above lit up. Esther wouldn't come. His last night living in this neighborhood was cold as Eskimos. Would his teacher, Miss Raidin, miss him? Hit and miss. . . . When he woke up, the sun had fainted. Bernice and Woody were near him, sleeping soundly. Esther was nowhere to be found. Coin knew that each one of them had dreamed of the past in a different way, because the last day was the last day. He would pack. He was alone. He rubbed his eyes. Esther was not there. Esther wouldn't come. He and Esther would never play Othello and Desdemona again. He would hate moving vans. Forever.

Coin felt that the change in his history was now, as he watched the empty moving van ride up to take away the family possessions to a strange place. All the kids were lined up for the leaving. The friends and neighbors were looking from their windows. The Foremans were moving away. From the window where his mother always had watched, Coin watched. The procession of furniture and the staples of his childhood went out on the backs of men who didn't realize what they carried, or cared. Their job was being done. Oh, he looked. There goes the lamp Agnes used to read to us by. In that lamp is Dickens's *Christmas Carol*, the favorite passage of his father's from Lamentations and Jeremiah, from the Bible; a chair came out, an ice cream chair. Woody and Oscar and he . . . him . . .

had got all those haircuts from Popa in that chair. They sure were messy cuts. Popa was trying to save money. Oh Lord. Now the table where all the meals were eaten. Three hundred thousand by accurate count. Mama had mastered all those lima beans and stews because of her love for them, and limped to the stove to fetch onto the table what she had sometimes accomplished on less than fifty cents. Then came the bed; the lowdown bed he and Woody had spent their nighttime lives on ever since they were born. When the movers brought out the bed his mother died in, Coin began to scratch.

In the bare room there was only one thing left: the seashell his father had given him. He needed that to hold against his ear and make voyages when things got too bad at home.

Coin noticed that in the new house, Miss Horwitz was always killing flies. She had a sure enough swatting eye. Folded newspapers were everywhere for the hunt. On the dining table, in the toilets, the sofas, the bedrooms. Flies were big game. And although screens had been sent for, he knew that she would swat at cats the same way she swatted flies. Yes, she went about the house with her folded newspaper, killing. She was patient. Sometimes she would wait three minutes at a time to watch a fly circle, inspect the dust on venetian blinds, finally land and fall dead when she hit accurately. Well, he thought to himself as he and Miss Horwitz were cleaning the second floor of the brownstone, there really wasn't anything wrong with killing flies *or* mosquitœs. *But* Miss Horwitz went about it as if she were killing people. Reminded him of the story Mrs. Quick was telling Agnes the other day about Deaconess Redmond.

"Lord," she had declared to Agnes, "you know Deaconess Redmond has landed in the Brooklyn Old Folks Home for the Aged. She made it all right. But nobody can stand her. You know about that eye she had to have taken out and had the glass one put in? Now you know what that old devil do at dinner-time when all the decrepit is sitting at the one table? Every night, chile, she sets down and, *after* grace has been uttered, she takes out that eye and drops it in her water glass like something for medicinal purposes. And there it sit at the bottom looking out of the water. Sometimes, they tell me, Deaconess Redmond rolls the glass around and the eye looks all around the table. I was there one evening, on invitation of course, and I could hardly eat for looking first at that empty eye socket screwed up like the devil's wink and then at the eye in the glass staring me down. Now you know, I declare, they ought to turn her out. Some of them folks haven't touched a bite in several days, and you know how old folks loves their vittles. They couldn't eat, chile. That eye were not on no sparrow, it were on them. Now you know it were. Listen, and that ain't all. One night when old Deaconess Redmond put the eye back in her socket upside down, no one would tell her. It served her

62

good and right." She and Agnes had roared together. "Mean, that Redmond, mean."

He wished Miss Horwitz had a glass eye. He'd
steal it and give it to Woody for his aggie collection.
He bet Woody would win many a game. Swat,
swat. She was at it again.

"Coin, look in that corner; you haven't cleaned
out the dust from there. Children nowadays don't
do anything thorough." Swat. "But you're learning.
By the time we get this place cleaned up, you'll be
able to hire yourself out as a parlor maid." And she
laughed, making the hissing sound through her
raisin teeth. He'd like to yank them out one day.
Swat! Swat!

Coin had to admit that it was a nice house
in a way. But you never felt like running through
it or talking loud. You felt all the time that
you had to sit up tall. It was a house you didn't
want to play games in. And if you said a bad word
the walls would tell on you. Then again there was
so much room. And it all had to be cleaned regular.
Three floors. Downstairs was the dining room and
kitchen and bathroom and a backyard. Agnes and
Miss Lucy were planning to turn that into a model
garden. No fun there. On the second floor was a big
living room and a back parlor. Upstairs was a bedroom for Agnes and Bernice, and behind that Miss
Lucy's room, then a storeroom and off from the
hall another bedroom. When he and Bernice were
inspecting the house for the first time, she said,
"Buckingham Palace, Your Royal Behindness!"

Everything in the new house started off badly. The first thing Coin had the nerve to do was to catch the cold of his life. Miss Horwitz, with her old black self, said he did it because he didn't want to work. There's where she lied. He'd had a paper route ever since the church burned down and had given most of the money to his father for the re-building fund. And he had collected horse manure to sell to people for their backyards since who-struck-john. Anyway, they made him stay in bed in the back parlor for three days. He was lucky that there was a radio by his bedside. He listened his time away.

On the third night about ten o'clock there was a mystery story after his heart. It was called "Who Killed Raoul?" Everybody was involved. There was one simple old lady. Raoul had been mean and bad to her, too. She put up with him without a fight. She said she knew he was evil but there was nothing she could do about it. One policeman, when he was questioning her, told her that as soon as she saw evil there was always something to be done. (You could at least call the police.) You had to rip it out or it would get a stranglehold on you that you couldn't break. And so on he went, scaring the old lady to death. She just sat in her wheelchair. Coin knew she hadn't done it because she was a cripple. The suspects were seven and there were clues everywhere. That was the trouble. Coin was dying with suspense. He couldn't wait for the end. Miss

Horwitz came in about five minutes before it was over and told Coin to turn that infernal thing off.

"I'm listening to a mystery, Miss Lucy."

"Mystery. I'll mystery you. Keeping the whole house awake and you pretending to be sick—sick my foot. You can fool Agnes some of the time or all of the time, but you can't fool me." And she snapped the switch off just as police whistles began to blow. The killer had been found.

Miss Horwitz stood there daring him to turn it on again. He could have died. Now he'd never know. He hated her forever for that; so he got a headache. But wait a minute, maybe somebody would invent that machine his junior high school teacher, Mr. Bransky, was always talking about. Mr. Bransky had the thought that every word that had been spoken on this earth was still in the air. All we needed was a machine like a radio, but more delicate, that could hear right beyond the sounds we made at the moment. It could relay to us exactly what the wife said to Alfred the Great when those cakes burned, Lincoln's Gettysbury Address, Robin Hood talking in Sherwood Forest, Shakespeare reading to Queen Elizabeth, Jesus Christ's Seven Last Words from the cross, his mother's final sigh, and maybe he could find out—who killed Raoul! The air air air must be so thick with talk, it was a wonder you could breathe. He could hardly breathe now. Maybe he'd die! That would fix Agnes and Miss Horwitz. He had a chance to die. *They* would be to blame. He'd fix their hides. But he went to sleep and woke up in the morning feeling fine, bless God and the hindmost.

Coin suspected that Bernice had a secret boy friend hidden somewhere in the streets of where they had lived before, and he was certain of it when that package arrived: Miss Bernice Foreman, from some old yesterday shop in Brownsville. There was no telling what people could get themselves into, especially sisters. So he stayed waiting for Bernice to return and open the package. Chile, he thought, come on home. And she sure did. Black and evil from something that had happened at school. She marched into the house like all the children of Israel were tramping on her tail.

"Bernice," he said softly, "there's a package for you."

"From Jehovah himself, I suppose." And she switched forward to her room up the stairs. He brought the neatly wrapped box to her.

"Don't come in here, I'm naked as a jaybird, leave it at the door," and she left it at that. Coin waited outside the door. There was a rattling of paper. At last she came out, dressed, with a squint smile.

"I got a present," she said, showing him a bottle of perfume that was open. She held it under her nose. "It's a sweet smell like glycerin and rose water together, only better." Then she shut the door in his face. He heard her humming. Be happy, he said to himself for her, be very happy.

Bernice had set her bottle of perfume smack in

the middle of the medicine closet on the top floor. Coin saw it looking proud there. But Miss Lucy used that bathroom. Something was going to happen and it did. One day later Miss Lucy came back from her job with products from the druggist. "Coin," she called, "help me place this mess." So Coin went to help. There were douche bags and Epsom salts, aspirin, foot powder, toenail scissors, fingernail polish, Sloan's liniment, and whatnot. There wasn't room for everything she had. He had just been playing a careless hand of three-handed whist with Bernice and Woody and wanted to hasten back as soon as possible. Also, Agnes had asked him to watch the food on the stove while she washed up downstairs.

"Now I suppose there ought to be enough space on *my* shelf for these few things." Well, there was, except for the Epsom salts that just wouldn't fit. Then Miss Lucy saw the perfume bottle. "Well, Coin," she said, "I know that you and Woody don't use this at this stage of the game, and Agnes refuses to use perfume. So that Bernice has had the rotten nerve to set her cheap perfume on my shelf. No place for my salts." She was beside herself when she called loud as kingdom come: "Bernice, Bernice, I want you to come up here this very minute." There was a long silence. "Bernice, you'd better get yourself up here before I tear the hide off you." So hollering, she stamped her foot and waited for Bernice. Miss Lucy breathed heavily, as if her breath were brown and thick and stiff. She stood tapping her foot until Bernice began mounting the steps. At the bottom, Agnes and Woody waited, wondering what all the matter was about. When Bernice was halfway up, Miss Lucy rushed to the bathroom and seized the bottle of perfume, rushed out again and yelled, "Stop where you are." Bernice stopped, too. Everything stopped. The house stood still. There was Bernice halfway up and Miss Lucy all the way up. Silence. They faced each other like in a duel. Pistols were on their minds.

"Well, Missy, I found your cheap, cheesy perfume on my shelf and no place to set my Epsom salts!" Bernice began to advance. "Stay where you are, my lady. Stop there." In her hand she held the perfume bottle. "I'm going to teach you the lesson of your black, selfish life." And Miss Lucy had the nerve to crash that bottle against the stairs—down it hit toward Bernice and landed in the middle of the stairs.

Agnes and Woody, at the foot of the stairs, looked thunderstruck. Bernice wailed long, hard, terrible and loud. It was the first present she had ever got from a boyfriend, Coin knew. She wept on the steps till Agnes went up and walked her down. Coin heard Bernice wailing in the dining room. Bernice sounded troubled in her inner mind. Lamentations 1:2. Coin remembered that passage because Reverend Brooks had taken his text from there at a funeral for a girl who everybody knew had sinned, and he was going to teach his congregation a lesson to "be engraved in their minds forever. . . . I will cut these words into the marble of this hour," he had shouted, "lest you forget that the world must be purified even in the hours of mourning for the death of this child who sinned, had life ripped from her womb and so died. Listen to Jeremiah! 'She weepeth sore in the night and her tears *are* on her cheeks: among all her lovers she hath none to comfort *her*: all her friends have dealt treacherously with her, they are become her enemies.' So I, your pastor, say, beware! Let not this happen unto any of thee. Let us pray." And the congregation bowed down their heads. But the girl's mother fainted, her father cried, her sisters crept out in shame, her brother tore the black band from his coat. And when the mess was over no member of the family was there to follow the coffin up the aisle to the hearse or to the grave.

In Agnes's and Bernice's room Coin thought these lessons out, sitting on the bed. Now he was almost fourteen years old and solutions were as far off as ever. When he had returned from his looking for Ferris he was a reformed fingernail biter. Now he started on his nails again with a vicious attack of teeth at nails, at Miss Lucy, at Agnes, at Death that had taken his mother and father and left him locked in the cell of his need, crying for understanding. His thoughts spun about in his brain making thick cobwebs there. How could he help Bernice? Or Woody? Or himself? Jeremiah, if he were here, would have been too wise to understand a boy who didn't know a seashell from a voyage. He spit a fingernail onto the bedspread; then he forced himself to doze.

Voices from the bathroom startled him awake. It was Agnes and Miss Lucy talking in the bathroom. Agnes's voice was calm and tight at the same time. Miss Lucy was a screamer. And, by the blowing of noses, he knew that they both were crying.

"Listen, Lucy, this is a home, a family, and you are a part of it. We went into this together because you wished it. I did too. Now if you aren't going to be one of us, I'll have to ask you to leave. These are my brothers and sister and I want them with me. I'm responsible for them. I love them in spite of any sacrifice. Don't try to come in here and hurt any one of them. What you did a little while ago was something I never dreamed I'd witness. But since it did happen, I wish it never to happen again or I'll despise you."

"Agnes, don't leave me. Please. I promise, I promise to be right. I couldn't live away from you." Tears like horses weeping hit his ears. And then: "They always get in *our* way, scuffing around the house."

Calmly, patiently, Agnes said, "This *is* their house, not yours or mine, really, but *theirs* and if you want to pull out of the bargain—pull out. I'll pay what you put in, somehow."

"I'll stay, Agnes. I'll try to be better. I'll try. But only . . . only don't be mad with me. Don't be mad. I'd kill myself if you were mad."

"Mad, I'm not mad. I'm thinking of Bernice crying her eyes out because the one thing that she had was smashed for no reason. You knew that boy had given it to her, and how much she cherished that poor, pathetic bottle of nothing. It won't be easy. Every day when she gets home from school the smell of his gift will come running to her heart." And she said, softly as leaves falling, "I remember Harry."

Miss Lucy's voice tried to be a mop swabbing up Agnes's wounds. "I'll fix dinner now. You lie down. Go inside, lie down, rest for a minute." When Agnes came into the bedroom, Coin knew she didn't know he was there. But somehow he couldn't move or speak. She went over to her dresser and picked up a bottle of her GLYCERIN AND ROSE WATER. He could hear the soft click of glass on glass as she placed it on Bernice's shelf.

What made him happy after all this time, was to know that Agnes was on their side, that she loved them and in her, Mama and Popa lived again. And that even in this house, maybe, their lives would grow again. When Agnes returned, she saw him.

"You know, Coin, I think you need some new trousers and shirts. Then you can visit your Esther again." Tears welled up quietly, softly in Coin's eyes. Perhaps the dark time was finished. GLYCERIN AND ROSE WATER! Forever.

Dinner that night was a feast. Miss Lucy had fixed the feast of the world on their table. There were fried chicken and rolls, green peas and rice, string beans, salad, and, at the last, ice cream and homemade cake. Even Bernice perked up. They ate as if it were kingdom come. Coin forgot about Miss Lucy's breath and smelled nothing but the food. The more he looked at Bernice, the less he had to worry about, the timetable of the house was on time. He didn't think too much of "Who Killed Raoul?" At the end of the meal, Miss Horwitz offered him coffee. Miss Horwitz could not have killed Raoul!

Chapter Four

Alone, Coin sat by Agnes's bedside waiting for her to die. He had sat there, it seemed, for the last two years waiting for her to die. He did not want her to die. He and Bernice would be the last of the Foremans at home. Oscar was only a shadow remembrance and the smell of old socks caked to unwashed feet. He hardly remembered Oscar's voice hissing between battered teeth, or the weight of his noise snoring in the back parlor on Berriman Street. Oscar couldn't even be found when his father died. The man from the reform school said he had run away, that they could not trace him, and between his teeth said that he didn't care. Oscar had never seemed like a brother. Woody had always been his brother, even when they stopped playing together, because Woody considered him a child and not old enough for the ways of his world. Woody was away, hardly wrote, and never came home for holidays. He didn't have time to put up or

73

down with Miss Lucy Horwitz and her keys. He had gotten out. Coin and Bernice and Agnes abided alone, locked together by approaching death and memories of love.

Miss Lucy had started locking doors the day Agnes had had her stroke with other complications, started locking doors, closets, chests, kept a separate shelf, with a webbed door and lock, in the icebox for her steaks and niceties, cheeses, charlotte russes, and whatnot, dared anyone to touch them. Miss Lucy had not only commenced locking doors, what was worse she attached tags with notes written on them in her spider handwriting: *If you resent closing doors, don't open them. Signed, Miss Lucy* (this was on the living room door). *I resent riffraff looking into my room: keep out. Signed, Miss Lucy* (this was tied to the knob on the door to her room). *This is my shelf, fend for yourselves. Signed, Miss Lucy* (this was pasted on the inside door of the ice box near her "foods"). *I detest cigarette butts in my garden beds. If God or the Devil had wanted you to smoke he would have put smokestacks in your head. Signed, Miss Lucy* (this was attached to stakes firmly driven into the ground near the flower beds in the backyard). *This china is for Sunday use, I resent chips.* Or, *These are the every-day dishes which you can use, which I did not chip. Signed, Miss Lucy* (these were pasted on the cupboards around the kitchen). *The hot water heater burns up money, bathe moderately or not at all. Signed, Miss Lucy* (on the heater in the cellar). The house was alarm-

74

ing with do's and don't's, with warnings and reproaches.

From the day Agnes was taken sick, Miss Lucy also began walking around in shoes that made no sound, and she appeared everywhere without notice. Even the steps didn't creak. She had experimented placing her weight scientifically. She was, unexpectedly, behind doors, in recesses, cooking, tending the garden, leaning over your shoulder, greeting the mailman, holding all letters to the light, turning down the hot water heater, hiding loot in bins in the cellar, turning out lights, gargling, sorting out dishes (cracked from the uncracked), even flushing her toilet without noise. She became their F.B.I. She was a ghost with flesh, an echo without sound, a fury in padded feet. She had nailed the windows in her room shut for all seasons. And the house began to smell of her armpits and breath.

Agnes lay before Coin now, unspeaking and unmoving, but he knew she could hear. Only her eyes spoke. They had become wide, solitary, ready for tears at all moments in the last two years. She seemed wrapped around by past voices and the life of the wounded, never to rise again. Coin waited for her to die. There was nothing else. Only, he thought, if he could ask questions of her and have answers, she would be relieved and ready to die, and he would be relieved and ready to go from this house.

Agnes stirred and Coin was alert to her. As he

bent over her bed she looked at him, telling of her temptation to leave, but not yet. Her eyes roved all around the room and then settled to his eyes. Perhaps she said, this is my legacy to you and Bernice; perhaps she said, help me in my need; perhaps she said, I wish I had stayed on Berriman Street. She looked at him blessed in health and tried to die, but she would not die. They nodded there together and finally slept with Coin's head resting near hers. Coin slept, almost blind with tiredness. He did not know what to do when she looked at him. He looked at her and then every which way. Silent night, unholy night. He lay there in the hectic feel of her illness because she was the Zion of his need and he was the Zion of her need. Brother and sister alone. Mama and Popa: Hello in the grave.

For the past two years, rest had been only the dreaming nightmare of his waking hours. It was as if a magician had turned his sleeping time inside out into awakening time, and both were the same. He recalled dreams of what had surely happened when awake as well as asleep. Now he slept, fogged with weariness, but he had heard, or thought he had heard, Miss Horwitz, Miss Lucy, Lucy, padding up to the bed he sat beside, speaking to the sister he lay beside, padding up on the rug, saying in a Dracula voice:

"Good morning, Agnes, you're restless, you didn't sleep much last night. Too bad, too bad. Why don't you give up, Agnes, give up? Look here, your brother has fallen asleep on you. Young people nowadays have no stamina. Well, I guess I'll go brew my coffee before I start my day . . . *my day*. . . ." As if Agnes had no day. And the end of the padding speech, "I guess I'll be forced to bury all you Foremans."

Then the cackle got low, or perhaps Coin was on the edges of sleep. In the morning he'd never know if Miss Lucy had spoken at 2:00 A.M. or 12:00 noon or if at all.

But one morning, after all those words had been recalled, he awoke, smelled coffee. Padded feet was moving around the kitchen fetching her "foods" with a noiseless conversation to—them. Her lips were moving, he could see, but the sound was secret from him. From his place he could spy *her* drinking *her* coffee up like a Dracula drinking the Foremans' blood in, sip by sip. There was a bitter and ugly secret in her eyes. He had learned to read eyes since the time Agnes could not speak. Now he knew that his dreams were true and the day's events true. They never really left off from each other.

The words in the mornings to Agnes were really what old Miss Horwitz had said. Perhaps she had said them to Agnes every morning. He shuddered. Shuddered, thinking of Agnes hearing, not being able to answer, Agnes spoken to that way by a friend who had planned a home with her and now . . . Agnes, O Agnes, turn your ears off! Should he tell Bernice and trouble her, or might it be better to let this secret rest with him. Bernice might be in deep trouble—trouble of her own.

Bernice was becoming a woman, and for once she had a steady boyfriend. He hoped she wasn't doing things with him to keep him as her steady. He knew, and Bernice knew, too, that there would not be many boyfriends in her life. Some way he wanted to protect her from Lamentations like in the Bible. Sometimes, finding Bernice crying by herself as she looked in the mirror at her dark, rusty face, he wondered wherever she would turn when Agnes was gone and they were at the icy mercy of Miss Lucy. And you couldn't comfort or take her out.

"I don't need my brothers to take me out to dances and the movies, I can find escorts of my own; thank you just the same, Coin. You're a swell brother. Go on back to your books, I can take care of myself."

And there she would stand weeping, lipstick unnoticed on her teeth, a lonely scowl in her eyes. Coin would tiptoe away. And in an hour or so she'd come downstairs with a joke, or singing as if mirth were her usual state.

Agnes lay quiet. He could tell she wanted the lights out, as if the darkness would prepare her for her future. Coin touched the switch and the streetlamp light shone through the blinds, casting prisoner stripes across his sister's body. Images of the past years living in this house moved in his mind and unfolded before him. The pictures seemed to move in slow motion, wobbly, as if the camera of his memory had recorded the scenes underwater in an echoey tank. That day, for instance, when he came home from his summer job in the shoe factory, and Bernice met him at the door and whispered to him before he had a chance to enter the inner hall.

"Coin, get yourself together."

"What's the matter, Bernice, I'm all right."

"Agnes ... Agnes has had a stroke and complications. It's bad. She can't talk or move." Oh my God, he had thought, what else, what else? The deaf and dumb and blind from the Kentucky train spoke again in semaphore. Poor Agnes. She had just paid the last payment on their first mortgage and they were supposed to celebrate that tonight. And now this, after all these years of work to put a roof over their heads. This had to happen. Bernice gave him one deep look and he knew she was thinking the same thing. She pressed his hand and ran her fingers over his cheek with delicate sympathy for both of them, for Agnes, for all the changes this would make in their already cut-down lives. As they turned to go in to see Agnes, Miss Horwitz stood before them. She must have gotten there by magic. But beside them she was. Her hair was pulled back fiercely into a bun exposing the every inch of her cigar-brown skin and her pointed cheekbones and her dagger eyes. Her lips were pressed into a line sharper than a knife.

"I'd like to see you both upstairs, now, at once."

"We'll be up after I've seen Agnes," Coin said tightly.

"You'd better hear what I have to say first. You

and Bernice. I think Agnes will wait," she said, and started up the stairs with them following. She went into her room and held the door for them to enter. Then she closed the door. It was like being inside of an asafetida bag. Nor did she ask them to sit down, but sat down herself, sucking her tongue. Finally she spoke. She slingshot her first remark to Bernice.

"How old are you, Bernice?"

"You know how old I am."

"I asked you a question, Miss."

"Eighteen."

"Well, at least you can't lie about that." Then it was Coin's turn. "How old are you, Coin?"

He was ready for her. "Older than you think."

"Oh, you can be as smart as you like but you'll both laugh on the other side of your black faces and nappy heads after you hear what I have to say! So pick your noses and fasten your shoes, my words are the ones you'll have to choose. That's what my mother told me when I was not your age, Bernice, but when I was ten years old. Ten black years old down in Virginia without a pot to piss in. And she sent me out to work for the folks in town who were the hardest and meanest in the county. So I was broken in when I was supposed to still be dreaming of Santa Claus coming down the chimney."

Coin felt that if he didn't get out of that room at once, he'd smother. His stomach began to screw tighter and tighter, and his eyes smarted in the quick air. Bernice spread her legs for support, and she looked back at Miss Lucy eye for eye.

Miss Lucy settled herself on her bed like a ramrod. Her upper body shot upwards, her breath reached him smelling of manure. The worst kind. And looking at her he knew she was putting out all the lights of her past friendship with his mother, Agnes or them. In that darkness she slung the arrows of her plans at them, arrows aimed so accurately they hit the marks in his heart.

"Now listen, I'm going to tell you something, and I'm going to ask you to do something. And if you don't wish to do what I'm asking, it won't make any difference. You're finished anyway. So it doesn't matter if you do or don't mind your p's and q's."

Her laugh came out ugly. It was a surprise to Coin that he felt sorry for her. Long ago he had heard a sermon preached from the pulpit in the Corinthian Baptist Church. The guest pastor for the summer had taken his text from the verse: "Once I was young but now I am old." Miss Lucy was old compared to him and Bernice. Let her spout and spout but time finally would inch her out. He couldn't tell what Bernice was thinking but whatever it was it had deep waters to it with hard-shelled fish.

Miss Lucy continued. "Neither one of you was around when your sister fell before this doorway, perspiring in her pain. She was nearly frying in the heat when I came along and got help to pick her up and lay her in the dining room and call a doctor for her distress. . . ."

Coin had been at work, Bernice had been at work. How in hell could they have helped when they could not be reached. (He didn't care what she had to say if he could only get out of the smell that was ruining his nose and his reason, that was aimed toward ruining his everything.) But that voice of Miss Lucy's, lined with manure, shot out urgently from the slit-pursed lips. She became almost soothing as smells dropped in her talk. Why did she have to whisper? You'd think she was trying to caress them with her plan.

"*I* talked with the doctor. Your sister needs a nurse with her all day. Constant attention day and night. I think that you, Bernice, and you, Coin, can attend to the night. But as you know I substitute-teach in the day. A nurse *is* needed. The hospital is out of the question. I can't give up this teaching for *your* sister. *Your* sister has told me more than often that hospitals would kill her. She formed the idea because *your* father chose to send her to a public ward when she contracted appendicitis—and the operation has led to *this*."

Her *this* tried to make her father guilty of Agnes's condition now.

"It was a colored doctor that recommended the hospital. Your father was a race man and *wrong*."

Coin felt something rising in Bernice. He wasn't afraid, but hoped that she wouldn't go too far. Bernice was as firm-footed as ever and her words came edged in determined black.

"My father," said Bernice, "my father was a good man. Anything he did, he did because it was right. I don't want to listen to you saying he caused Agnes to be here now. She can't talk and she can't move. But whatever happened, my father didn't cause it."

"I've listened to you longer than I care to, Miss Uppity. I've listened to you since I realized you were the hussy you are. You had better keep your black mouth shut or I'll shut it for you."

Miss Lucy had arisen. No, she had not gotten up, she arose her full height as if she was nine and a half feet tall. She stalked Bernice into a position. They stood there aiming at each other in slow motion. Coin suddenly realized that he had to act. If they came together he would have to part them. If they stayed apart he would have to quiet them, each in their own corner. And, downstairs, there was Agnes, listening, perhaps, to the sharp battle and not able to counsel them apart. Coin raised his voice to reach the ceiling of their emotions. "Stop, stop. You'll die if you don't stop." Miss Horwitz let down her arms and Bernice pulled her teeth in. Miss Lucy sagged her body to her bed, Bernice went back to her position with legs spread apart. The room seethed as the women panted in their eye-for-eye and tooth-for-tooth. Silence hung seaweed and slime animals onto the dark draperies of their lives. They remained motionless. Miss Lucy and Bernice stared at each other until Miss Lucy slit her mouth into words again.

Sitting down to her bed again, she was as composed as if the encounter had not happened.

"Your sister needs a nurse. This I will pay for." This she would pay for. No one would pay for his sister besides himself and Bernice! But even while he had said it, he knew he was not capable of paying the day-by-day horror of the principal cash of illness. Bernice, standing by his side, had no resources to truly help.

They both listened, watching Miss Horwitz, with her advantage, as she hit them over the head with their need and her desire. She seemed to creep into her sheets when she put forward the next question.

"Do you love your sister?"

Who could hesitate? "You know we do. You know that, don't you realize that?" Bernice's voice was soft as lipstick, red in conviction, thick and soft, sentimental as Christmas. She bowed her head, leaning toward him. Now he was the man of the house and had to make decisions.

"I'm glad to hear you say this, Bernice," Miss Lucy uttered. "Your sister and I . . . now that she can't speak it's harder for me to speak. She must be taken care of somehow. . . ."

Bernice spoke in the fire of the situation. "Thank you very much, we'll take care of her. Coin and I will."

Miss Horwitz jerked up taller than time. Her body seemed a tower before them. Her breath was smothering. The electricity of her thinking lighted the darkness of their responsibility. She cut through the cushions of their years together. She was crafty and cunning. Coin knew he could not match anything she was about to say. And Agnes downstairs was silent, suffering in the agony of her paralysis.

"Now you realize," Miss Horwitz began her recital, "your sister and me . . . I . . . have this house together. You realize that she needs care, food, and the whatnots of life while she lives. You are young in age and experience. We have bought this house together and have dwelt in it together, with *you*. Now Agnes is very sick, sick, I mean death-near sick. And she needs care. I will provide the nurse by day if you will provide the providence by night, if you know what I mean. The nurse costs sixty-five dollars. Hard, precious, real dollars. Take it or leave it. I get the house after, instead of you. I hope you understand . . . or I will see that your sister is shipped to a city hospital, where she will surely die at once."

The hard, cold science of Miss Lucy's voice had to be listened to and borne with.

Bernice spoke first. "Miss Lucy, can Coin and me . . . I . . . speak together before we give you an answer?" Bernice looked at Coin, beseeching help, bolster, even a word. Coin knew there was no word to save Agnes or keep her living without Miss Lucy. He couldn't give Bernice a sign. The signs had been given long ago. Their dice had been loaded when Popa died and a throw either way now would result the same.

"I'm waiting for your answer." Miss Horwitz had become absolutely black. The three of them stood in the triangle of the problem. Did a house matter when Agnes was at stake? Did anything matter except the last rites of sacrifice to keep Agnes alive minutes, days, years, hours? Anything was better than the procession again to a new grave. Also, deep, deep down in him he felt that Agnes had become his mother, that Agnes had slaved for a house for them, and to give it up would be saving her life inches longer. A house meant a shelter, oh, more than a shelter ... he had wanted a home; that was what Agnes wanted, too. This house had meant a roof only, but it was her life now. There was no decision to be made.

"I'm waiting for your answer," Miss Lucy repeated.

Bernice started toward the door. She walked blind.

"Miss Bernice, you haven't signed the papers. Here." Miss Lucy thrust legal papers toward them.

"No, I haven't signed no papers. Don't open your mouth to correct my grammar; I ain't signed and I aren't gonna sign no papers. How's that for your English, teacher." Bernice poked her tongue out like the flame of what was going on inside her, flickered it toward Miss Lucy.

"I think you are making a mistake, Bernice. Agnes doesn't deserve this from you."

Bernice tore around in a mighty wrath. Her teeth began to bite the air with her words. "Oh, Miss Lucy, oh, Miss Lucy, ooo, ooo, ooo. I've got my eyes on you. I know what you want. Don't come scumming around me with your approves or disapproves. I got a furnace of Hell in my mind to burn you in. And what's more, don't go correcting my English. I speak to you the way I do because I want to match your dirty mind. You aren't fooling anybody. Your unnatural desires. Now I've said it and you can put it in your pipe and smoke it. Third, you're not going to put me out of the house my sister worked for and paid for, halfway, with you. My brother here can say what he pleases, but I'm determined, bent and determined, to do what I please and know is right. You can put that into your righteous pipe and smoke it, too ... too and again." The unsounded sound of Miss Lucy's answer was evident in the room. He just didn't know what to do in this hatchet duel. He couldn't cope with these women. Their fury made a dent in his heart.

Finally, Miss Horwitz spoke with the authority of those who had the upper hand that was able to reach for money that was there, solid and low enough for them to grab. Her voice was a bass force. It was quiet, steady and sharp. "Bernice, either you'll sign or get out this minute. This is my word, my last one."

They fought downstairs to Agnes's bed without a word. There they stood around Agnes.

Coin caught Bernice looking lonely, ashy-black

and canceled. She had started a revolt without ammunition to shoot it through. Then the strange thing happened that made them all stand still, suspended, alert, startled, mystified, and eclipsed. A scream from the bed made them all look up straight. Agnes was sitting up, screaming. Her body was a shooting thing in the air above the bed. Miss Lucy, Coin, and Bernice rushed closer, in unison for once. They settled by the bedside like blackbirds halting in air. Then Agnes spoke her first and last words since the stroke. "No," she said, "Bernice stays here." Agnes's exertion was incredible, was an effort of love and lost hope. Her body rested exhausted in the chaos of her feeling.

Coin felt empty, empty. Lucy pushed to the bed in certainty. She leaned to a whispering position and delivered words, like all the gunshots of wars in the world, at Agnes. Bernice seemed to crucify herself to the wall. Miss Lucy issued her announcement clean and straight into the tragic bed.

"All right, Agnes, all right. But let me tell you something, let me tell you all something. Bernice will be shoved out of here as soon as you die. I say," and she turned to Bernice, "as soon as your sister dies, you'll be out."

Bernice was as quiet as down cotton when she spoke. "Miss Lucy, I will stay with my sister and tend her with Coin until Hell freezes over."

"Don't wait for that," Miss Lucy replied. "Hell is perverse." Then she twisted her body around and padded out into the hall. Her only sound came from her backside. Coin held his nose.

Tears spouted from Agnes's eyes in floods; floods that issued, he was sure, from this now and the past and even from the dark she must see before her. Bernice walked to rock Agnes in her arms like a baby doll. Coin crossed to the other side of the bed. The three of them stared at the steps Miss Lucy was ascending. A slit smile was sewed to her lips as she turned back to watch the triple weeping below. "Tomorrow morning, at nine A.M., the witnesses will be here to witness your signatures." Then she walked out of sight into the doings in her room.

"I'll sign, Agnes, I'll sign," Bernice wept.

Agnes breathed with slow insistence. Coin knew she was still alive and went back to the thoughts that filled him. Death was around like all the tasks of life that must be fulfilled. He reckoned that it was the final night and so he determined to stay awake. The nurse, Miss Gertie Adams, had left hours before. He was glad about this. She had been an ally with Miss Lucy. She was one of the enemy, doing everything, exact, in the white of her calling.

One day Coin had come in and noticed Miss Adams in the kitchen preparing an injection for Agnes. He watched as she measured whatever dose the doctor had ordered. As he got nearer the kitchen, the door to the large closet of the kitchen opened silently and Miss Lucy was there, smiling away. Miss Adams turned. Coin hid. There was

Miss Lucy beckoning. As the nurse went over she pressed her voice down and said, "Put more in, if the poor woman is suffering, put more in; it's better that way." The door to the pantry closet closed and Miss Lucy disappeared behind it. Coin watched the nurse with care to see what she would do. But Miss Adams measured the usual amount into the vial and walked toward the bed. He saw that nothing out of the way happened. Agnes was safe for the moment.

Coin became a spy. He started watching everything and everybody who approached his sister, even the doctor, but especially Miss Lucy.

The day that cornered him was when he was sitting beside Agnes's bed thinking of nothing in particular. From the kitchen there came laughter. Not happy laughter; it issued forth confidential, squeezed, and secret. As he turned his head, Miss Adams and Miss Lucy were, he saw, exchanging humorous, hilarious mutterings over the stove where the injection needles were heating.

Vicious alley cats, perched on the fences and defenses of his mind, began fighting the conspiracy going on in the kitchen. He didn't know what to do, but he had to fight against the kitchen plan of Lucy. He had walked to them and, shielded by the strength of his own presence, said that he would give the injection to Agnes. The women were silent for a moment. Presently the nurse let him have the instruments. He went into the dining room and pantomimed the gestures of injection, but he gave her nothing and laid the plate aside. When they were not looking he squirted out the liquid.

Every day, then, Coin watched to see that they didn't attempt to kill. He gave up school. His whole life was oriented toward the deathbed. And when Bernice came home she let him sleep and woke him up when it was necessary for her to go to bed. The two years had crawled by, concentrated on Agnes' bed. *Bed* had become the watchword of their lives.

He remembered mostly the cruel behavior of Miss Lucy and Miss Adams, in the period when they were smilers and laughers. Whenever they saw him or Bernice, they would break into secret smiles or downright laughter. The kitchen was the battleground of their mirth.

The first Christmas after Agnes took sick he recalled as a miserable thing. As he woke up, he felt Miss Horwitz behind him, breathing down his neck. She was twinkling, had even stuck some holly in her dyed rabbit coat. Agnes looked at them with eyes so tired and strained that Coin thought she would die in a minute. Miss Horwitz must have seen Agnes's state because she got brighter and talked sweeter. Even her breath didn't seem so bad.

"Merry Christmas, dear Agnes," she sparkled toward the bed, "and Coin," she said, "your gift is in the icebox under my shelf." Then she kissed Agnes on the forehead and went out silently.

A while later, when he was in the kitchen, he remembered what Miss Lucy had said. He didn't want a gift particularly, but was interested in what was on Miss Lucy's mind. When he scanned the icebox he found it, his Christmas gift. It was wrapped in red paper with a tag addressed to him. There it was—an old piece of cheese half eaten away, smelling sour. Anger arose in him, shot directly to the top of his brain. He turned on the radio so that Agnes could hear the carols and have some kind of holiday. Bernice came in and began straightening up. The nurse, Miss Adams, was not due that day. Coin went upstairs and sat on his bed; the old piece of cheese was still in his hand. Without realizing what he was going to do, he rushed to Miss Lucy's room and with all his strength, smashed the smell in his hand against the window. The crash of glass in the silent house sounded louder than the crackle of hell fire. And he was glad. If Miss Lucy had been there he would have smashed it against her pussy eyes.

He panted silently, thinking of a plan to kill her. In his mind the necessity to kill her expanded through his body like yeast. First he got out of that room. He went downstairs to the living room door; it was locked. (No Christmas tree this year.) He sat down on the steps and began to plot; he conjured up all the detective stories he'd read, he saw mystery movies rush before his eyes, newspaper stories digested in the past rose up in sensational, vivid print. He concentrated on poisons, nooses, drowning, hand-choking, pushing-downstairs, knife wounds, lye-throwing, snakebites, injection of air, smotherings. If he could remember vividly each act of violence, he would select one way of killing Miss Lucy that would be foolproof for all cops and detectives, judges, juries; all who didn't understand the wreck of abiding in this house that waited with him for death and would survive.

The carols from the radio downstairs jerked him to.

Hark, the herald angels sing,
Glory to the newborn king. . . .

Deep down he knew that the worst thing Miss Lucy had effected was to darken his mind, paint his mind with horror colors, pad sin on his floors, decorate his inner room with infidelity, hypocrisy, and dishonor. She had made him wish to kill.

Silent night, holy night,
All is calm, all is bright. . . .

The songs pulled him together and told him what his direction was, could be. . . . How in the world he let that woman pull him onto the rack of her sore soul! Christ was born in straw wilderness with a carpenter father and a magic mother. Yes, all was not calm here, all was not bright, but he had his sisters and Miss Lucy could not take them away from him. Let Miss Lucy die in her own time. He wanted to keep his straight line clean. And so he nodded again until the street lamp went out and the prisoner stripes across Agnes disappeared.

There wasn't the sound of morning anywhere,

not upstairs, not outside, nowhere. Stillness had entered every corner. Without reason his heart began to thump, thump, thump. Then he heard the milkman leave the milk and the gate clicked, then a cat began to cry, then the first light of morning came through the blinds ... then he knew. He knew the task was finished. Slowly he got up and looked at Agnes. Her face had let go years of living. She lay there secret, so alone and calm. Finally she knew the mystery they all had to know. Coin couldn't cry now. Six months ago he had done that, begging her to try to live. His tears had fallen, shaking to the floor; his heart had been full of glass at that time, and tinkled in that afternoon light. She had glanced at him with the terrible, final look of those who could not defend their lives. Six months ago he had felt that weeping was a need. Now nothing was necessary, not even the need of love. He sat there, wondering if death was still in the room. Patches of faint, early sun came here and there on the walls and chairs. The light circled Agnes's face. He bent over and closed her eyes from everything. Then he went upstairs to tell Bernice and Miss Lucy.

Bernice didn't cry or anything. She only said, "We've got things to do."

Miss Lucy went into her closet and, yelling into her funky clothes, she threw her hands up, caught at the clothes and let her weight bring coats, dresses, hats, scarves down onto her. She flayed her arms in the midst of disorder. Finally she crept out, disorder shaking her face. The tears were terrible to see. Her eyes chose a place to speak to. She spoke with all the innards of her body. She wrestled in disaster. She pleaded with the quick air of the room.

"You left me," she cried, "you had the nerve to do it. You've gone away. I damn you and I resent God. How could you leave me alone?"

She lay there like a carpet on the floor. Coin would have stepped on her but she was moaning into the floor in animal grunts, asking Agnes to live again, asking forgiveness, asking another chance. When Bernice appeared at the door, he was lifting Miss Lucy up and she whispered for them to take her down to see Agnes. Step by step they struggled below until the three of them reached the bed. When Coin looked, Agnes had turned sixteen. Her skin was clear and her expression was poised in her lips like the surprise of every spring. Miss Lucy faced the bed and gazed. The voice he heard was a scratching, it was a holler and a ratty noise that hit the walls and the china closet, hit Bernice's face, slapped his. Miss Horwitz's voice rammed into the morning and killed last night's stars, birds that survived through the winter; it was a bedlam. "Get," she said, "get," she screamed, "that thing out of here." She pointed toward Agnes's body and then fainted, falling into Bernice's arms. Bernice let the weight drop through her arms to the floor.

Now Agnes was dead. Would his house ever graduate to weddings and births?

Chapter Five

Bringgiiiiing, the bell went, bringgging, bringgggggg. Coin jerked up from the parlor chair where he had fallen into a first blind sleep after Undertaker Ward had come and taken Agnes from the house. Briniiiing, briiining, the bell insisted, bringiiiiiing, the bell insisted. Miss Lucy's padded footsteps were on the stairs and before he could get to the door, she was at the foot hurrying to answer the bell. He stood by the stairwell as Miss Lucy opened the door cautiously. He saw Mrs. Quick there, trying to thrust her great bosoms in. She got into the vestibule in spite of Miss Lucy's strength. She panted her question. "The neighbors tell me something happened here last night. How is Agnes Foreman?"

Miss Lucy Horwitz wrapped her kimono tighter and answered in a voice that would, could have frozen the South Sea Islands: "I saw them taking something out of here in a long wicker backet some time ago," and tried to shut the inner door. Mrs. Quick pushed her way in. She looked straight into Miss Lucy's eyes and said, "I thought so. I'd like to see Coin or Bernice." Miss Lucy stood there unmoving. "I would like to *see the children,*" shot Mrs. Quick. Lucy maintained a concrete silence.

"Oh, get," said Mrs. Quick, "get out of my way," and pushed her way into the inner hall. "Now," she faced Miss Lucy, "where are those children?"

Then Coin came forward. He felt lost and deserted and alone as he stood before Mrs. Quick's mountain of courage and sympathy. Yes, and he was happy that she was there.

Mrs. Quick shot a look at Miss Lucy that meant business. "Well," she said, "Coin and me are going to have a few words ... alone." She stood her ground as Miss Lucy padded up the stairs. Glancing back only once with a Sphinx smile on her face, she looked them up and down, then continued her way up as if she were ready for Paris or Rome, with a rabbit fur tossed around her neck.

Mrs. Quick led him into the parlor, sat down on the sofa and adjusted herself before she said, "What are your plans now, chile?"

"I don't know exactly, Mrs. Quick, but I'll find somewhere to go."

"Somewhere to go." She rammed up bolt tight. "You got the house right here, now you know. Half of it was Agnes's. I'll-find-somewhere-to-go, you talking like you've got no sense a-tall."

"It's different from what you think."

"T'ain't nothing different from what I think. If Miss Lucy's trying any of her tricks, I will declare them before God and all of Brooklyn will know it. What does Bernice think about all of this?"

"All of what, Mrs. Quick?"

"Whatever you're talking about, chile."

"I'm . . . I'm not talking about anything, Mrs. Quick. I . . . I was just thinking about Agnes all alone at Undertaker Ward's." He couldn't think of himself or Bernice, only of how his sister was put out of her house, the house she had worked for and loved so well. Put out before she was buried. Perhaps it wasn't important to be buried from your home, but he knew it would have been important to Agnes and Mama and Popa. He would ask Miss Lucy about it presently.

"What!" exclaimed Mrs. Quick. "The body's not to lie in state here in her own home that she worked to make this beauty attraction of Brooklyn! Now you know that ain't right. It's hateful and unchristian, sinful, and not according to the tradition of your family. And my having to press the front bell until the skin nearly wore off my finger to get in to express the sympathies of my heart, now you know that's almost cause for a suit, yes it is." She panted and put her hand over her heart. "If I was a weaker woman, now you know, I'd need the smelling salts. Lord, gospel-Savior, this is a mess. Coin, you reckon there's some aromatic spirits of ammonia in this house so I can breathe in my nerves together?"

Coin hadn't been listening. He was concentrating on the idea that after he was born his mother got a stroke because he had been born and the strain had been too much for her, and now Agnes was dead because she had tried to make a home for him and Bernice and Woody. He felt guilty in every muscle of his spirit. Agnes could be married to Harry, his mother would be living, and his father would be presiding over the deacons in church. He felt a great black crepe on his arm being drawn like a tourniquet. He was the chief mourner at the deaths he had caused. Then in the background he heard Mrs. Quick going on about spirits of ammonia; he heard Miss Lucy pacing the floor upstairs, Bernice at the sewing machine downstairs, making a black dress. Deep inside him he knew he wasn't guilty. Things beyond his control had just happened. You'd have to go a long way back to find the cause that caused what happened before the one before the last and so on and on, back and back. There was no beginning and there would be no end. Who was to blame? Who was to blame? Who was to blame? It stuck in his head. Finding an answer was like trying to win on a pinball machine in Luna Park. He was feeling sorry for himself and he knew it. He'd better stop all that.

"Coin, you know, now don't you, that you have my sympathy? I wouldn't be brooding like that, crying inside. Let them tears come out, son, and lay your head on my bosom."

He started to rise. "I'll get the ammonia, Mrs. Quick."

"I don't need it now, son. You're the one and Bernice."

"No, I'll go. . . ."

Mrs. Quick got a little bit stern and pulled him down. "Lay your head on my bosom, I said. . . ."

Coin didn't know what to do, but two sharp rings of the bell saved him from sitting down again. Miss Lucy was coming down. Mrs. Quick took him aside and in a hurried whisper told him that if anything happened to let her know, that she had something in the back of her head. "Don't worry about a place to stay if worse comes to worse." Three of the neighbors had been let in. Mrs. Quick thrust Coin back a little way.

"You know I got your interest at heart, at my heart, chile, now you know. I loved your mother and I *loved* your father. They would want me to be keeping my weather's eye on you. Remember that. I will be in and out of here the next days." And she kissed Coin near his mouth with energy. "The Lord is my master, and thou shalt not want." Then she switched herself past the neighbors, sniffed at Miss Lucy Horwitz, and made a rapid exit with her handkerchief to her eyes, her bosoms puffed high.

Coin went to his room, scuffing the floor deliberately as he walked along. He at once sought his seashell, snatched it and held it against his ear. Squatting on the floor, he listened. Always since he lived in this house the shell had been his armor against the civil wars of the house. Once against his ear, bickerings dropped into the bottom of the sea, barbed-wire quarrels were eaten by the sharks, hurts were comforted by mermaids, his algebra was solved by sea lions, electric snakes volted shocks (thousands a minute) into Miss Lucy's yellow teeth and she shut up, went into the deep; Mama and Popa kissed in silver-green water: between them they held a crepe paper rose that never wilted and smelled of the garden of Eden; Coin ate fruit resting on coral, reveled in the rushes of fishes around his toes and, like Columbus, found new sea lands and Indian fish with seaweed feathers and harpoons of gold to split the enemy in half. And then he'd make a voyage to Mesopotamia.

So now again he picked up the shell to escape the dangers and decisions to come. He held the shell against his ear and listened for the old, unreal escape. There was sound there, sure enough. He held it away and then put it close and the roar was like nothing he had ever heard. Hurricanes, tempests, reached him and then parted, leaving him within a squall of real voices like talk over a faulty telephone. It had never been like this before, not with his shell, not with him. The last months rattled in his ears:

"Miss Bernice, Miss Bernice, what do you mean drinking coffee out of the Chinese cups on a business day? Those are the company dishes, Missy."

"We never have any company, Miss Lucy."

"Shut your black mouth, Miss, and get those dishes back on the shelf."

"You're black, too, and don't you go calling me that, Miss Shoe Polish, Miss Greasy Stove." Bernice's voice spoke like hard-shelled crabs. Their voices tangled in seaweed. Another conversation covered their sound:

"Well, Agnes, now let me tell you, this Jew was trying to jew me down and I refused to be moved and told him if he wanted to make a sale he'd better get himself and his race in line. . . ."

Coin heard himself saying, "Don't talk like that, Miss Lucy, we've got some real swell Jewish friends and if they cheat us, everyone else does too, and all races got cheats in them. . . ."

"Agnes, ask him to leave the table."

"I can't do that, Lucy, I agree with him."

"Agree with him, agree with him. I believe you're becoming a Communist, Agnes Foreman."

He heard the dirt pounding his mother's coffin to seal her in. He heard Miss Lucy bending over Agnes's bed whispering like grasshoppers humming:

"You're not going to get well, Agnes, not this time, you're not goin'. . . ."

He heard the terrible shouting in church when a sinner was brought forward weeping like an animal . . . SOMEBODY'S KNOCKING AT YOUR DOOR. . . .

He heard everything that was terrible at once, and above and below the sounds of the past there was the hurricane underneath the sea washing all

103

the words together, slapping them around, tearing them apart. The fish were screaming. Cries of DO, DON'T, THOU SHALL, THOU SHAN'T, YOU'RE BAD, YOU'RE GOOD, YOU'LL END UP IN THE GUTTER, YOU FAILED YOUR ALGEBRA: slap, slap, COIN, MAMA'S DYING ON THE CROSS, POPA, DIED ON THE CROSS, YOU'RE GONNA DIE ON THE CROSS and the whole congregation of the sea sang: WHERE SHALL YOU GO, WHERE SHALL YOU GO, WHERE SHALL YOU GO, TO EASE YOUR TROUBLIN' MIND. . . .

Bernice and Miss Horwitz and neighbors were bending over him and he was rolling on the floor. The seashell had failed him, his mind had failed him. There was no escape now. And he couldn't stop crying even when Bernice bent over him in her new black dress and tried to rock him in her arms. The pins that held the dress together stuck him here and there, and he almost smashed the seashell of escape against Miss Lucy's dark and ugly face.

"Bernice," Lucy shouted, "calm your brother down. I don't want tantrums in *my* house. This is disgraceful." Bernice shot her a look of pity.

"Come on, Coin," he heard Bernice saying almost like a song, "come on, kiddo, and lie down. Rest a little bit. You'll be all right, come on now."

Coin got up slowly, holding the seashell. Now he was face to face with Miss Lucy. She held out both hands as if to help him. "No, no," he rejected her, "no."

"Coin," Miss Lucy said, "I didn't mean to be unkind, I . . . I only wanted to make you snap out of it."

Bernice looked her straight in the eye. "You could have helped, you really could have, but you. . . ." Her voice got quiet, "I wish you had a heart, Miss Lucy, I always wished you had one." The neighbors stepped aside as Coin and Bernice walked from the room.

One thing, he realized as he lay on the bed (with Bernice sewing her dress, sitting, with dark concentration, across the room), was that his seashell days were over. He would always keep this humped and beautiful prophecy his father had given him. But he knew that whatever sounds came from it, whatever it suggested to him, was in his own mind. Accepting this, finally he was able to sleep.

That night, at Undertaker Ward's Funeral Home, Coin and Bernice stood before Agnes's casket. Bernice had selected a white organdy shroud that made Agnes look like a bride or a graduate or an older girl in her confirmation dress. Bernice, in black, at eighteen looked much older than Agnes.

Bernice's voice was quiet, matter-of-fact. Underneath the control Coin heard the heartbreaking sounds she would not let out. "I decided on white, Coin, because she looks so young. She looks like the picture of Mama when she married. Poor, poor dear Agnes. You know what she told me while she could still speak? She said, 'Bernice, everything hasn't always been peaches and cream for me but I've had some good times . . . the only thing I regret is that I never, never had a man. I always wanted to know what it would be like. I don't know . . . sex . . . well, I just wonder what I missed. . . .' She told me to take care of myself and that was about the last thing she said."

"Are you going to stay with Miss Horwitz, Bernice, after the funeral, I mean?"

"No, kiddo, I'm going to live with one of my girl friends. I couldn't stand another minute in that house without Agnes. I'll get a typing job or something. And you know I might even get married." He noticed her swallow hard. "And you, Coin, what are your plans?"

"Maybe I'll go into the navy. I've always wanted to travel. I'll have to stay at home until I enlist. I can't think of anything else."

"Get away as soon as you can. I wish I could help but I'm not Agnes." They both turned to the coffin. "The orchid Woody sent is nice, isn't it?" There was a long pause. Coin wanted Woody there. He should have been there. Bernice answered his thoughts.

"At least he escaped and that's good. Don't feel lonely, badly, about Woody, Coin. He made his decision and left. He might just make it."

People had begun coming in. So Coin and Bernice moved away from the casket to let them see the bride, the confirmation girl, the virgin, their sister with Woody's orchid pinned to her dead white, glowing white shroud. Miss Lucy was nowhere to be seen.

When Coin and Bernice came home that night the whole place was lighted and there were two painters changing the colors of the walls. Miss Lucy was walking about, talking to herself: "I'll get them to move the sofa into the left corner and those pictures will have to come down.... Those children have scuffed the floors until they're a sight. I'll make a note to call the scrapers tomorrow.... Agnes's clothes, I'll leave them for Bernice to get together. Won't she look a sight in them...." She acted like she didn't even see them as she strode about with her pad and pencil. "I better plan to get some bars put up at those windows with all this trash starting to move into the neighborhood, they'll murder me in my bed.... Maybe I better not go to the funeral tomorrow, the painters might run off with everything I've got. Agnes won't notice if I'm not there."

The painters brushed on as if they didn't hear her. She looked up at one of them. "Watch out there, you didn't get that spot. I'm not paying you to skip."

"Aw look, lady, it's late."

"Don't aw-look lady me! Do your job and keep your mouth shut if you expect to be paid."

Coin wasn't exactly amazed; what he realized was that he couldn't stay in the house one minute after he left the cemetery. Where in hell could he go? Right now he'd have to go to bed. But the seashell couldn't help him. That was the worst of it. Bernice had her plan. Woody had had his plan. Mary and Martha had wept for Jesus, but who would see to him? Then he felt guilty thinking about himself and not Agnes whose life was finished before it had begun. And again: he was so goddamned sick of death. Caskets and before them, the sick. Was he crazy as Miss Lucy? Would he survive? Well, after tomorrow he'd have to do something. So he put on his pajamas (he didn't even touch the seashell). He slept.

The next morning, the day of the funeral, the painters were covering up lives in that house, sealing in the joys and sorrows, disguising the Foremans' world. Miss Lucy came down the stairs with her hand gripping the bannister, possessing the wood, the paint, the furniture polish on it. She was dressed in the blackest black in the world. The only thing she didn't have was a veil but she held a long black handkerchief like a final benediction. She passed the new paint and the painters. Only once did she glance up. "The ceiling in my room needs a second coat of calcimine." With this remark she walked to the first car. Bernice refused to get in with her; she and Coin got into the second car and let Miss Lucy ride away.

When the burial was over, the limousines took them to the house. Bernice had already packed her bag; she went in and came out in a matter of seconds. Coin waited for her on the sidewalk and ran up the front stoop as she came out with the heavy luggage. "You'll be here for a few days and I'll send my address to you. Look out for the mails because that old bitch might try to foul us up."

Coin found a taxi for her. Before she got in, she turned. "We're the last, kiddo, always let me know where you are. I'll help you when I can."

"Yes, Bernice." They looked at each other. Agnes had held them together. Bernice's dress really looked homemade. So what!

"The meter's going, lady," the driver said.

"I'm ready to go, driver, I'm ready." She got in. Coin bit his longest fingernail.

The cab drove off so rapidly, he hardly had time to wave.

He stood there on the sidewalk. There was a clap of thunder and angle lightning. He watched down the street the cab had gone. He stood there even when the rain came down in long, hard needles to sting him. Miss Lucy came to the stoop. He felt her behind him. Her voice turned him around. "If the lightning strikes you, don't blame it on me." He looked into the black-gray sky. His clothes were drenched and so was his heart. He turned and went up the steps, smelled the new paint as he walked through the door.

For the next few mornings, after Miss Lucy left for work, he stood by the gate waiting for the mailman to bring the letter from Bernice. He didn't think about anything very much except how he was going to get out of this house and survive. There was still the money left that the church members had thrust into his hand before and after the funeral. School wouldn't be open for a while so he didn't have to think about that, thank goodness. Each morning the mailman would come swinging down the street. Most of the envelopes, he could see before he opened them, were cards of sympathy. No nothing from Bernice. He began to worry about her in a vague way but deep down he knew she was all right, just not situated yet. On the fifth day, as he was sorting the sympathy cards at the gate, he saw Mrs. Quick puffing up the street. She walked like she had jumping jacks in her stomach and between her bosoms. Even before she got to him she began to talk.

"Lord, chile, now you know I got all your problems settled. Well, here I am with the news." She reached the gate with her millionaire smile.

"Hello, Mrs. Quick." Opening the gate, he asked her if she would come into the house.

"I ain't going into that house, Coin, now you know, I'm bent and determined to get me to Heaven before I enter Hell." And she laughed as fat as you please. "We can just stand here at this here gate and chew the rag. Or better still, let's sit on the stoop."

Coin opened the gate and they sat on the brownstone steps. She didn't waste any time. "You remember Mrs. Elsa Dominican, the rich white lady on McDonough Street. She has that gingerbread brownstone. It's right next to the house where I have a room, now you know." She poked her elbow into his ribs and let out a juicy laugh. "Now Mrs. Dominican got no case against the colored, only she said to me the other day that they was moving in so fast the property was likely to go down, and she was getting old and whatnot and thought she might sell since she could see the handwriting on the wall. 'Colored handwriting,' I said to myself." And she shouted laughter again. "Well, the upshot is that she's done moved out. Left a spare room on the second floor with living equipment in it for someone to stay in to show folks the house who might want to buy it. Since I'm living next door she give me the key to the house. Now you know that white woman trust me!"

Coin wondered what Mrs. Quick was getting at but he fidgeted with the sympathy cards.

"Don't be impatient, chile, I'll come to the point before you know who-struck-john, now you reckon I will?"

"I reckon you will, Mrs. Quick."

"Well, ain't you something. You got answers sharp as a razor in a barber hand." She giggled at her wit and jabbed him in his ribs so hard the cards fell down. As she was picking them up he noticed her pick a card from between her bosoms.

"This is the address and I'm next door. You can have that room in Mrs. Dominican's house until a colored buyer comes along. All you have to do is to let them in and show them around. And that is that. I got no personal interest in it myself. I just thought you might be anxious and ready to clear out of here." She patted his thigh and rose. "Think about the room and come around tomorrow and we can talk."

"Thanks, Mrs. Quick, I'll see you tomorrow."

After Mrs. Quick left he went into the house and began to pack. He didn't know if he should talk to Miss Horwitz or just leave after he saw the place Mrs. Quick had described. Then again he hesitated; suppose Bernice's letter would arrive! If he missed it, how would he ever find her? Tomorrow morning he would wait again.

He woke up softly the next day like a bird that had slept on tiptoe, untired, waiting for the dew. Each action was planned. He washed his face carefully at least six times, he kneaded the tonic into his hair, he brushed his teeth until they shone more than five times white, then he took a farewell bath. When he emerged to go into his room Miss Lucy met him in the narrow hall. There was something triumphant and ragged about her, yet all the new paint seemed to well out of her body and clothes.

"I saw your bags packed. You're leaving. Well, don't say I put you out." Then she gave a dry cough. "This paint gets into the throat and you've got to cough it out." She held a large handkerchief to her mouth and harked up some large mess into

112

it. "These painters nowadays must use a turpentine fit to kill. I can't abide this smell. Well, so here I am with new walls and a cough. . . . One thing pays or the other. Good-bye, and remember you always got a home here." Then she sneezed, she sneezed and harked and spit into the handkerchief and laughed, wheezing, as she let him out with the bag. There was a kind of pus in her eyes and the same kind of look he remembered from when he was on the lookout long ago watching the church burning down, and he thought he saw thorns for Jesus in her oyster eyes. He heard the lock click.

Then he was standing by the gate, waiting for the mailman, with another past ended in new paint and a series of coughs and sneezes. Soon the postman came along nodding that there was nothing for the house. Coin picked up his bag with deliberation and started toward McDonough Street and Mrs. Quick's proposal. Bernice had left him; Agnes slept to the tune of dry hymns; Mama and Popa believed in the dazzling life after death.

Coin stopped in front of Mrs. Dominican's house on McDonough Street. It was an old Victorian Brooklyn wonder, looking part church, part Masonic Hall, part retreat for old ladies who pared their fingernails with special concentration. It looked, too, like the home of injured bats who beat their wings against moldy walls, a house where tired rodents died in the walls. Coin gazed at a new disaster and felt he could conquer it. At least it was a dead place; he would exert his skill to make it

113

live. Mrs. Quick, alert as usual, poked her head out of the window next door and beckoned him up. "Honey," she yelled, "leave your belongings right there. Now you know ain't nobody gonna snatch them. Nobody in his right mind, that is."

The room where Mrs. Quick lived was all green velvet portieres and Morris chairs for fat behinds. On the walls were mounted painted china platters with huge roses and cherubs laughing between the leaves. There were pictures of Christ: *Christ in His Cradle, Christ before the Elders, Christ Walking the Waters, Christ Turning Water to Wine, Christ Moaning in the Garden, Christ on the Cross.* In the center of the room there was a round table covered in a green velvet cloth with cotton balls at the end. In the middle there was wax fruit: grapes from Lebanon, figs from Jerusalem, apples from the Garden of Gethsemane, pears from Bethlehem. All of this was under a glass dome looking sacred, oiled to a shiny glow.

"Come in, boy. Welcome to my Mount of Olives. Hee, hee, hee, hee," Mrs. Quick laughed, "ha, ha, ha."

Coin was looking around the room. "I'm happy, now you know I am, to see you gazing at my pictures. I've got Jesus all around *hanging* up. And now you're here I have one of his little lambs." She hugged him. He felt uncomfortable but knew that she meant everything to help him in his need. "Now sit down on this soft sofa here and let us have the talk. Don't be fidgety, Coin, nobody's gonna steal

114

your possessions. This is a respectable neighborhood. Mrs. Dominican's *former* neighborhood. Most everyone around here is white."

Coin settled on the sofa and began to feel at ease. "Now as I said, Mrs. Dominican's house is right next door (ain't she got the pretty name, one of the prettiest names I know, Elsa Dominican; sounds like her husband was head of the Metropolitan Life Insurance; maybe he was, for all I know, that house is that grand). Well, now, this is what I propose. You stay on the second floor in that one room which is furnished—there's not another lick of furniture in the place—and after you gets home from school all you have to do is listen for the bell of people inquiring to buy this property and show them around. Here's the key and you can take your evening meal with me. If that's all right with you. With thee." And she poked him in the ribs harder than the day before. "I see you looking at that picture of *Christ Turning Water into Wine*. Would you fancy some wine? I'm not a drinking woman but I keep some wine for hospitality and *communion* with friends, now you know!" She moved toward a highboy across the room. "Ain't that sofa softer than new bread? Indeed it is."

Mrs. Quick was reaching for some glasses. "Thank you, Mrs. Quick, but I don't think I care for wine." Coin said this as gently as he could so as not to hurt her feelings.

"Well, just as you like, you being most seventeen

and all. I don't drink it myself regular but when guests come I think it's nice. . . ."

"Mrs. Quick, I don't want to interrupt but could I take my things up to the room? I feel a little tired."

"Lord, honey, now you know I should have thought of that myself. Of course, yes indeed. Follow me. I don't need no wine. I only drinks it with my friends or as the blood of my Savior." She opened the door and led the way downstairs to the street. "Now there are your luggage sittin' where you left it. I told you this were a white neighborhood!"

So with his bags Coin entered another house, older than the others but newer to him than tomorrow's sunrise. Mrs. Quick followed close behind breathing satisfaction. As they approached the door to the room that was to be his, she went ahead and opened it. "Here it is. There it is. Strawberry-colored, fit to eat."

Coin put down his bags. He looked around. Red furniture stuffed the room, the rug was so thick it rose from the floor. The cherry-red draperies blocked the windows. The bed was covered in Satan scarlet. It was all red of every shade. Coin felt he was in a special prepared hell. And the cloth was heavy and you felt that you must feel it, or taste it like blood-soaked, dried bread. He was in for something all right. Also there was something mysterious, he felt, about the room to the left of the entrance. It was shut off by double sliding doors when every other door was open.

"The room that was closed downstairs, Mrs. Quick, is that a special place?"

"Ask me no questions and I'll tell you no lies," she answered without hesitating. "No, honey, I'm making jokes, that there room is where Mrs. Dominican has stored a host of stuff and she asked me to keep the keys to her kingdom, now you know, I'm a guardian, yes I am! We will just write curiosity off our list. I've got some greens and fatback gurgling on the stove. You come over presently and we'll have ourselves that dish along with corn bread *and* communion. Lord, have the good mercy to come over, amen." Her behinds said the sentence as she switched out of the door.

The sunset made his red room a torch; all the furniture was lit up. As he started to unpack, he felt himself grow hot. So he went to the tap, in the corner behind a screen, and drank glasses of water before he threw the heavy covers off the bed and tried to sleep. Mrs. Quick was at her window across the way. He thought he saw her throw him a wink. He determined to sleep. And he did.

The greens and fatback would have to wait. He dreamed of fatback, and Agnes turning over in her unwanted grave, and Miss Horwitz testing the weight and density of paint, and there was Bernice pressing her belly to have a child. His sleep and the dreams held until the red room and morning woke him up. At first he couldn't figure out where he was. All the wrinkled red. In his Bible mind he suddenly felt like he was Jonah in the belly of the whale. He began to fight the covers and pound the mattress and pull at the draperies. Then he looked out the window and into Mrs. Quick's window next door. And there she was, smiling behind the glass like a moving negative. Everything came into focus slowly. Excitement died down and he felt himself dozing into sleep again. Then there was a muted ringing sound that died out and another rose up and another, then another. His body shot upright in the bed. He felt like an enemy had come. The ringing continued, even and insistent, muffled; he realized that it was a telephone. But where was it? He scrambled everywhere, looked into the closet, behind the draperies, underneath the bed. The sound kept on, steady and padded. He kept on looking until he thought he'd lose his mind. This was a giant, frightening mess. Then on the table beside the bed he saw one of those quilted things Agnes called a tea cozy, in the form of a cock, that rich people used to cover teapots to keep the tea hot. He leaped at the quilted cock, lifted it up and there was the telephone! He was so mad he wanted to strike it as if the sound were a living thing. Instead he lifted the receiver and answered, "Hello."

"Hello, son, I thought you were out of your mind not answering when I knew right well you were there."

"I couldn't locate the phone, Mrs. Quick." He still felt scared, as if he'd been through a supernatural experience.

The voice came back at him chuckling. "I should

118

have told you about that *cock*. It just slipped my mind. I should remember these things for my age. Well, are you comfortable and all? I missed you for the greens and fatback, but you know I understands and all that. A young man needs his sleep. He sure *needs* the *bed*." And her laugh came over so loud he held the receiver away from his ear a little. "Well, I know there ain't been no callers to see the house today, since you just woke up. Go on back to bed now that you know where the cock is located at, and then come on over presently and eat with me."

Before he could answer she had hung up. There was nothing to do but wash and dress, get by Miss Lucy's to meet the mailman, and return to greens and fatback for breakfast.

There was something wrong somewhere in spite of how kind Mrs. Quick was and the soft comfort of his new room. But he couldn't put his finger on it, decided that he was still too anxious about hearing from Bernice and having no real place to live. His new red room with a telephone under a bird was out of the movies and besides he'd be leaving soon. He didn't belong anywhere. Dangling. He was dangling like a puppet without anyone controlling the strings. He began to think of how to get his shirts washed and pressed, where he would eat when Mrs. Quick's hospitality was over. Maybe he could get to Aunt Harriet, but her hands were tied with keeping her blind brother, Uncle Troy. And even though he wanted to belong to somebody and some place, he felt like he didn't want to keep saying thank you forever to anyone. He had a place to stay and, blessed God, tomorrow would be a new day and anything could happen. He stopped short, tracing the shadow of a tree. Damn it, he thought, he'd have to stop thinking like the old sisters in church. Bless God. What in hell did that mean? God was blessed already. God controlled the world *and* Heaven, God needed to bless him! He was sitting up there with manna and milk and honey and Jesus Christ to run the errands, let alone St. Peter and the rest. Just as he got to thinking deeply in this way, he spied the mailman near Miss Lucy's and broke into a trot. He was panting when he reached the house.

"Good Lord," said the mailman, "you'd think you had some important letter on the way." The Lord again, thought Coin. Jesus! Everybody's on the Bible kick.

"I hope I have," replied Coin, not meaning to be fresh.

"I think I've got something here for you. Yes, I have." And he handed Coin a letter as he said, "So long, boy."

Coin wouldn't look at it for two and a half blocks. Finally, he couldn't help it, stopped short and ripped the letter down the side, turned it over for the signature. And sure enough he read, "Your loving sister, Bernice." He wanted to cry even before he read the message. She said that she was OK and placed at the above address, she asked him to be careful and thought it might be a good idea if he went into the navy. Since he had some education he might make a yeoman and not have to go into cooks and bakers, where most Negroes had to go. She put a temporary address down but cautioned him that she might not be there long. She was thinking of moving soon. Then there was a strange Bernice sentence: "I have something strange and precious to do and when I do it, I will be OK and write to you or find you wherever you are."

He put the letter in his back pocket wondering if all women were mysterious and darkly favored with extra sight. Bernice, with her hints of beauty, with her wisdom and positive hate of Miss Lucy and all that; Miss Lucy, with her black calm and determination; Mrs. Quick, anxious to make him her son, laughing the Old Testament into his life with the New Testament, to make him comfortable. He wondered if Agnes was mysterious, too, but her secret was buried. His mother was the only angel he could look homeward to. If she were living, she would wash out all the socks and pants of his mind and make them glow on the line where pure suns would dry them. As he went down the street to Mrs. Dominican's house, the letter from Bernice whisked against his ass.

This day was white and yellow; Coin didn't want the dark property of his mind to darken it. He chuckled, but right now he'd like to go to a bar where they were serving whiskey highballs and the devil take the hindmost!

Back in the red room, he'd no sooner gotten into his bed than the telephone bell began to ring. He lifted the tea cozy cock to answer it. Of course it was Mrs. Quick.

"Listen, chile, now you know I don't want to bother you but I'm bringing some folks in to look the rooms over there. This time I'll take them over the place since I'm free and all, and the next time I'll call on you. I just wanted you to know that if you heard footsteps or *anything*, I got everything controlled. Weren't those fatbacks and greens from down home?" She rushed out laughter and hung up immediately.

Coin lay on the bed and read Bernice's letter again. He listened for sounds downstairs but there was nothing to be heard. They were probably discussing matters, so he dozed off. When he woke up this time he was used to the room, so he didn't feel strange in it.

After he had brushed his teeth and washed his face, he decided to look at the house he was to show people around. Might as well start at the front door, he thought, as he went downstairs to the first floor. Just as well start here, and he looked to his left at the double doors where Mrs. Dominican had stored some wares. "Oh, shoot," he muttered, "those things are not my business." But some feeling inside him prompted him to go back and, in spite of the fact that he knew that the doors were locked and barred, when he pushed them apart, expecting to have a struggle, lo and behold they

122

opened as smooth as you please. He was confronted with a large, naked woman. All the confined flesh unfolded over hips and rippled in thighs, behind, rippled in legs; her breasts were the size of Fourth-of-July balloons beginning to inflate, her hair had grease-chaos on it. On an army cot lay a man naked, with his business at attention, and on the floor was a fifth of whiskey with two glasses guarding it. The woman's belly was a dark brown, watermelon-sized jellyfish. The unashamed man stroked his desire.

"Huh," was all she said without surprise.

"I'm looking for Mrs. Quick," was all he could manage.

"She next door, if you interested," and fat hands, with dime-store rings, shut the doors until they rang together. He was flabbergasted. Where was Mrs. Dominican's storage? The lock on the door? Where *was* he? Who should he call; who could he alarm? Mrs. Quick was a pillar of the church, a practical nurse and his bosom friend.

The trip upstairs was a slow one, pull, pull, up. The house where he was guardian! Someone had stolen Mrs. Dominican's storage. And there was just a cot in the room that should have been jammed with treasures of the Brooklyn world! Only a naked woman and man rested there with a whiskey bottle and two glasses. What was he to make of that! He couldn't make nothing of it. So he lifted the tea cozy and called Mrs. Quick's number. She answered at once in a voice as gay as pink.

"What you got on your mind, sonny chile?"

"Well, I don't know what I've got on my mind, but that front room's empty except for a cot and some whiskey and a naked man and woman."

"What!" was the reply. "I'll be right over. You sure haven't been drinking any of that water my Lord changed into wine."

"I haven't been drinking even water."

"Your sister's death has loaded you with dreams. Well bless my soul. Now this is something. I'll be right over. Isn't this something!" She hung up like she was anxious to put her dress on.

He met her in the front hall. The sliding doors were closed to the room on the left. She hustled in in a white Hoover apron, her nurse's cap starched on her head, and those bosoms panting and pausing under her chin. "Now where's this thing now, this orgy going on in this house *you* and I is protecting?"

Coin opened the double doors and they both looked in. The room was as bare as a bunion. There was nothing there. Not smell, not cot, nor whiskey, nor man, nor woman, not a thing but bare walls and sunshine streaming in, laughing, at his folly.

"But . . . but," stammered Coin, "where is the storage stuff?"

"Storage stuff? Why, Mrs. Dominican give orders and probably had that moved away while you were pursuing the streets this early morning. This morning."

"Excuse me for bothering you. Maybe I was . . .

well, maybe I was dreaming. I'm away from home, you know, and subject to being wrong."

"Boy, don't you know I know that. Sleep a little bit more and arise refreshed in mind. I will be watching you from my window, praise your naps, I'll be here. Ain't that a fancy tea cozy, just like Mrs. Dominican! And she got it right at her bed." She switched from the room.

What in hell was this? He was sure he saw that man and woman in the room; he was certain of the whiskey bottle and a strange smell of bodies. Was what Mrs. Quick said about his new and sudden change responsible for his not being able to tell what he had seen from what he had dreamt? After all, he hadn't even known where he was when he woke up that very morning. He would go out for a walk, perhaps a walk would be just the thing to help him see the details that were blurred now. And one thing he would do as he went out was to open the double doors to the room downstairs and see that they stayed open for his own peace of mind and for the safety of the house and the trust Mrs. Quick had put on him. He went down and parted the doors. The room was the same, bare as a bunion. He thought he'd lower the shades so that the sun wouldn't fade the damask walls more than was necessary. As he reached for the fingerpull, he slipped. And there at his feet was the evidence that made him know that he was right. He scuffed the translucent, worm-colored mass off his shoe. Not feeling disgust or anger or anything, he went upstairs and took a bath. Lying in the tub he tried to think nothing. As he dried himself, he knew that he was a sixteen-year-old, sad fool; he would have to do something or else drift along to nothing. He dressed very slowly. He pulled the draperies together in a sudden impulse and sat down in darkness on the bed.

Mrs. Quick had tried to help him and herself but she was using him as blind. Using Mrs. Dominican's house. Using the urgent desires of others. Here she was, his friend, slicing his life for her own concern. Who would understand it? Should he get in touch with Mrs. Dominican? But where was she? And how could he ask Mrs. Quick when she had declared that he had dreamed the whole thing up? It was a chewing-gum tangle if there ever was one. He couldn't very well go to Mrs. Quick with the evidence he had found and dangle that filth before her face. Imagine this whole nighttime mess in the Brooklyn day. He seemed powerless to act without the advice of sister or mother or father to give assurance to act. And anyway, he would have been ashamed to tell them in the first place. Now he couldn't even sleep the experience off. Some tattoo needle had traced the whole thing in his mind: a tattoo of sex and whiskey and hot flesh unashamed. Oh yes, he was on his own in the hurricane waters of the room.

As he started to pack, no water of understanding parted to let him through. Understanding to him now didn't mean knowledge but acceptance. He had the knowledge all right! The preacher had said once that the fathers had eaten a sour grape and their children's teeth were set on edge. His teeth were on edge, that was sure. But the only sour grape his father had eaten was poverty. He did know exactly why he began to laugh. He had been the master of a whorehouse for a few hours. What was he doing there even now? Did he always have to drift to be forced into dwelling places of sin and corruption? Or were they everywhere? He stopped laughing when his eyes fell on the great pink roses set in the deep, red rug. Well, he had to face it: he had come to this garden alone but the dew was not on these roses.

Paraphrasing the hymn he had learned as a child sobered him. He continued to pack. And for once he would act on his own. The next destination would be the Carlton Avenue Y.M.C.A., and then he would go to the Navy Recruiting Station near Borough Hall and find out how soon he could enlist and see the country and the world. His seashell could not be all wrong.

Chapter Six

Coin, on the upper deck of the U.S.S. *Commodore*, watched the sailors. They milled around, waved their arms, talked in wild disconnected language, singing, whistling, screaming across to each other, adjusting ties, hats, playing harmonicas, singing snatches of songs from home. The ship seemed suddenly to have been settled by starched, white birds fallen out of the sky like thousands of Icaruses, surprised at the climax of their destination. The Italian sun shone on their uniforms; their eyes flashed off brilliance like stars. The sailors leaned far over the railings, pointing to Vesuvius, the one familiar landmark they had been told of from kindergarten to Eight-B. They had even seen it in Saturday afternoon serials: Pearl White balancing at the edge of the dangerous crater. They seemed to want to fly to it as if it were a roosting place for their hidden homesickness.

The excitement was too much for Coin. He had

been up earlier than anybody to [...]
bor. Now, for a few minutes, j[...]
landed, he wanted to be alone. He wa[...]
tory, away from the horrors of home. [...]
scenic view arrested him. He was use[...]
shouting living of Brooklyn and Manhattan,[...]
the jumping of his nerves in concrete subways,[...]
bors of skyscrapers. He would have to learn to slow
down.

The deck below was just about deserted. It was
shadowy there. Finding the coolest bench, he lay
down, adjusted his uniform for a minimum of wrin-
kling and half dozed. The fellows had been pretty
good. His reading so much had set him away from
them. He had not made any particular friend or belonged to a single group. He had been on the edges
looking in. Because he was the only colored fellow
who was a yeoman, he felt special; the others probably felt he was special, too. Sometimes he wished
he had gone into cooks and bakers below, where
the Negro sailors mostly were. He would have been
laughing. Company of your own kind. He was his
own kind. It didn't really matter; he would have
been solitary in any company. Well, so, everyone
was more or less polite even if he wasn't included.
For a moment, in his doze, he got on his high horse
and thought self-righteously that hardly any of
them read Dante or Shakespeare or Dickens or poetry, or anything for that matter. He dozed, lonely,
waiting for the whistle of furlough to sound. There
were voices suddenly here and there as sailors saun-

tered by. Coin paid no attention. Sleeping in the shadowy light of sun is sweet, sleeping in this sun is right.

"You's a good boy when you sleep, but you very seldom sleep."

Nothing, he murmured to himself. It's a dream.

"I say you's a good boy when you sleep, but you very seldom sleep. Here you are sleeping *now*. If you's a good boy, Coin, you better rise up from there to greet my morning light!"

The voice was laughing. But in half-sleep commands only meant stand up. He bolted up, saluting with one hand and rubbing his eyes with the other. He was awake, peering. Seeing that it was only a cooks-and-bakers, he said, "Leave me alone, man. Can't somebody leave me to myself?"

There was a tall brown boy in front of him, in whites, with a smile on his face, blowing nonchalant breath over his fingernails and rubbing them on his insignia.

"I know you from somewhere," Coin heard himself saying in a voice as small as a sleepy peewee.

"I thought you was going to visit me in Madison," the boy answered with a candy-soft chuckle.

Coin's mind raced out of sleep. Then Coin rushed toward him and, in the collision, threw his arms about the whites, rocking, rocking in the embrace. He held the honeysuckle of his days in Washington, D.C. in his arms. His loneliness shed off and the sun cloaked them. I have a friend, I have a friend again. The harbor, this ship, everything was a festival to him now. If he could stay like this forever, he could never die!

"Oh Ferris, Ferris, Ferris, oh. . . ." Golden Ferris, golden laugh.

Ferris was alert. "Don't put your arms around me *in* public, folks will think we're funny."

"Funny?" Coin was so happy he could only repeat Ferris's word.

"Yeah, funny, you know, queer, queens, gay, sissy, fairy, faggot, man-lovers."

"Oh no," said Coin retreating, tears beginning. "We're friends, friends. You're my friend."

"Well, boy, you better learn where to demonstrate."

Coin really didn't hear a thing. Ferris was here. They were in Italy and he would not be lonely. Ferris. Oh, Ferris, remember when you went away, I tried to follow. Ferris, don't notice the tears in my eyes. Ferris, laugh for me.

"Let's go up on deck," Coin said. He was ready to view the world now. With Ferris by his side, giggling. With Ferris he watched the pale colors of the old world washing cordially up the hills of Naples into the sky. Underneath them the ship began to churn into the harbor.

"You should've been down there with us, Coin. Man, we had some greens and fatback and fun." Coin saw his past lonely days on the ship. If he had wandered and looked they would have been Ferris-days instead.

"I wish I had known you were on this ship."

"Well, we stayed mostly where *they* thought we belonged. So that was that." Ferris looked Coin up and down. "Well, you got the yeoman's stripe, anyhow. I never did get my crow. I sure got the jim crow." He laughed.

There was silence between them as the ship kept chugging, moving into the docks. The sea was not exactly blue, it was all the colors of blue mixed with green in patches. And the sun made the colors move. His heart moved, his mind stood still. Ferris had grown so tall. He was neat and straight and his skin shone from within. His eyes were the same, too, sharp black and white. (They made him think of confetti.) His laughter and high spirits made Coin forget the past when he was hidden in the closets of his life, hitting against the old dead clothes of childhood.

As they went back up to the main deck to get their furlough cards, Ferris asked Coin where he was going to spend his time. Coin hadn't the slightest idea. Ferris knew of an island sweet as honey in the honeycomb. "Plenty of fun and girls. Lord, they say the girls bat their eyes like baseballs. All you got to do is run. And after a while you have a homer."

At the top of the stairs there was an empty space. Ferris headed for it, Coin following. Putting his arm casually around Coin, Ferris asked, "Do you have *all* your money on you, boy, because these Italians are as treacherous, as treacherous, boy, as swamp eels and as slippery."

"Sure, Ferris, I haven't spent a cent beyond cigarettes and maybe a few books."

"You ain't been gambling?"

"Gambling? Oh no."

"We gonna be right good friends again." Ferris hit him on the back. "We better get out our credentials and pull ourselves together for this Naples. I heard it's a man-trap and a woman-trap and a whiskey-trap. Must be nice!" Hurriedly he said again: "You got your money *on* you?"

Coin asked, "Are you broke, Ferris?"

"Me, broke? Boy, I'm just about everything else except broke. You want me to keep your package of change, you look so scarey-like?"

"Thanks, I know you gonna look after me but everything I got's in my stomach belt and safe, safe and sound."

"Just so you got it on you, that's the main thing. They say these Naples folks got the X-ray eye. I'm only trying to protect you." He put his arm around Coin and pressed him shoulder to shoulder so hard Coin felt the belt around his stomach move.

"Don't," whispered Coin. "They'll say what you said about funny."

"Worry about that?" joked Ferris. "It ain't necessary to worry about nothing, not even skiddledy-do, when you with me, if you got long greens and Uncle Sam's crow on your arm."

Coin was content. Ferris knew everything and

everything was what Coin didn't know. So he followed his friend, admiring the swagger in his sailor-deck stride and the sun shining even from his shoes, talking to the deck in challenge.

As soon as they landed and were processed, they headed for the Galleria Umberto, a place with a ceiling that glassed over shops of all descriptions and where bars were scattered in every free place. Coin felt dazed from looking, from being in so strange an atmosphere.

"Ferris, can't we sit down and have a Coke or something?"

"Sure we can have a Coke. Did you come to Italy to have a Coke?"

"No," replied Coin in a small voice.

"Then order us some brandy. Wait a minute," said Ferris. He walked toward a distant sailor.

The sailor Ferris returned with had hair like disheveled seaweed; he was brown as an ocean stone; his waist was slim and he was a bower and a smiler with eyes that called but never answered. Ferris sat down and poured himself the biggest brandy in the world, content and lording himself. He seemed to say: here I am. He looked around the Galleria with grand style. He had not looted the world but looked as though he had.

"Horace," Ferris announced, "Horace and Coin, I got an idea. Let's all get the tattoo."

Coin didn't want any tattoo but Ferris was bent and determined, so he said yes and went with Ferris and the seaweed boy to a place in the Galleria that smelled of old bathclothes and the insides of rummage-sale shoes. Curtained walls in brown and moss gray reminded him of dog colors and burnt bread. She was old, that proprietress. The fat of her face creased like cooked suet when she spoke to them. Her assistant had a mouth like a needle piercing you as he answered her. The darkness in there clipped at Coin as he entered. Ferris had loused him up. Loused up or not, he was here, in a tent of darkness. The old woman didn't say a thing; just sat in her chair, a mound of ruined flesh begging your pardon and at the same time holding out her hand. The old man was like smoke from the ruin. The five of them paused waiting. When the old man smiled, showing particles of teeth, Ferris said, "Tattoo."

"We want the tattoo!" he accented. Action began. The man began sharpening needles, the woman took down a box off a shelf marked *Inglese* and held it out to the three of them. Ferris's face lit up.

"I tell you what, we close our eyes after I jiggle up this box and take whatever card we pick and have what it says nicked on us and don't show what we got on our arms until we get outside. You all game?" Horace and Coin looked at each other and finally nodded OK. The old man and the woman laughed as if they understood English. Maybe they did. The laughter was a joke between them, frightening as the Galleria, positive as garlic; it smelled of conspiracy to Coin.

"You first, Coin," Ferris said. Coin took out a card. "Don't look, boy, just give it to the man." Coin gave it.

The man glanced at the card. As he laughed his teeth looked like pebbles glinting in his mouth. He beckoned to Coin to sit down, rubbed Coin's left arm with alcohol and got to work. At first the needle hurt sharp but he wouldn't let on before Horace and Ferris. Then he got used to the sharpness in his arm, relaxed and took the treatment. If he winced he knew Ferris wouldn't do it and he would be alone with this scar. So he was very quiet, anxious, still, until the man said, *"Finito," without* his smile. The old woman came over to gaze at him like a cross-eyed Sphinx.

"Bene, bene." She looked at the wet arm and moved away. Coin got up and Ferris took the vacant seat. Then the old woman sat in a corner of darkness, folding and unfolding her skirt. Coin wouldn't look at his arm. It felt numb. He had pledged and fulfilled his word. He watched the man needle Ferris. Ferris got up and Horace took his place. They waited together. The woman filled the shadows with sighs. The man took up the needle again. Horace shook his seaweed head, crying. The old man staccatoed the message into the boy's arm. Coin and Ferris didn't look at each other.

It was done. *Finito!*

The cigarettes they had all smoked loaded the air. The smell of the man's hair, the woman's arm-

137

pits, the ink, alcohol, was too much for Coin. He raised his eyes from the floor to say, "Let's go."

Ferris paid the woman and they went out into the Galleria again. Coin saw the faces of the old man and woman staring deaf and dumb through the window, watching with mute hilarity.

"What you got on your arm, boy?" Ferris asked the seaweed sailor. And Ferris looked. "Suicide," Ferris pronounced. The words were written in Horace's arm in clear curlicues.

Ferris looked at Coin's arm. "Death," Ferris said. "Death is clearly on your arm." Coin looked at his numb arm for the first time. Death was there all right in red, white, and blue.

"Poison," Coin answered to Ferris when he and Horace looked at Ferris's left arm.

Ferris whooped a laugh. "Poison, suicide, death!"

But they returned to their table in the Galleria with sober faces. Ferris ordered more brandy and went off with Horace. He was leaving for a moment, he said, as if he owned Naples and had caused all the eruptions of Vesuvius. Coin sat silent while the pain in his arm called.

Presently a waiter appeared with a tray. He set down a bottle of brandy, soda, a bowl of ice, and went away. Coin looked for Ferris among the promenading crowds. There was no Ferris. Again he glanced around. The mass of people set his nerves jumping. He would have to go. Where? It

138

was Ferris who knew the island. If he left the bottle, somebody would snatch it up. Who would help him? The police? He was silly to look for security. He looked around for assurances. There were none. Everybody seemed poured into his own wine or whatever, and alert as yardbirds. Sailors. Why weren't there any sailors? United States sailors! Any uniform he recognized would serve to get him straight. He looked around again for Ferris. All he saw were girls, dark and ripe as hothouse grapes, staring at him, at others, at any audience. There were boys, too, right out of paintings, stroking one hand up their trousers, combing head-hair down with the other hand. Old men whispered to the girls and sometimes walked out with them. Under his nose, vendors with trays of rings and watches, cameos, all false jewelry of Bible size, tried to gesture him into buying what he had nobody in the world to give, didn't want himself.

Where was Ferris? Death was written on his arm. He was afraid. He was alone, without a place to sleep, left in a city where crime was natural and the smiles of welcome flashed for devious purposes. He was not prepared for anything except what the navy had taught him or what Ferris had promised. This furlough would be a gasser.

The rattle of the city, heard from the Galleria, grated harshly. He poured a brandy, was happy for the warmth. He noticed a blond boy in blue jeans standing at a distance, eyeing his table. From what he could see the boy was about fourteen and at the end of his rope. He walked to Coin's table and sat down as if he had been invited.

"Oh, oh," sighed Coin, "what shall I do now?"

Ferris would know. But Ferris was God knows where. Not here. If he ran away there would be no island and no Ferris to wait for. Coin sat tight and waited for the boy to say something.

"Hello, Mister."

"Hello," Coin heard himself say anxiously.

"What you drinking?"

Coin answered, "Brandy."

"Can I have some?"

"No, you're too young." The boy's head flew back and all the blond curls of his head told Coin he, himself, was the fool.

"I'll order a Coke for you," was all he managed.

"Thank you," the boy answered. "May I have a cigarette?"

"You're too young."

The boy pulled out a pack of Italian cigarettes. "Won't you have one?" People were watching and laughing and nudging one another to see who would win. Coin pulled out his own cigarette. The boy lit it. Where's Ferris? I want to leave, get away.

"Thanks," Coin said. The boy smiled as Coin smoked without inhaling.

The boy finally said, "You got a girl?" Without waiting for an answer he continued, "You can have a fine Swedish girl, seventeen, and you don't have to pay unless you like it."

He didn't want anything except to be with his

friend in this wild city where the sea splashed up shells, boys, prostitutes.

"No."

The boy leaned over smiling: "How about me?" He shed the Mediterranean Sea over Coin. Who does he think I am?

"Thank you. No. Definite no! I've got to leave now." Coin stood. The waiter came running after he put a tip in lire into a waiting dish.

"That's exactly three cents," the boy said.

Coin fished out a 100-lire note and walked away. The boy followed him. As Coin crossed the street to his hotel, the boy stretched out his hand.

"What's that for?"

Directly the boy answered: "Because I've been so charming." Coin carelessly gave him some lire and entered his hotel. Then he went back to the table at the Galleria.

Ferris had better come back. Everybody, he felt, was looking at him and at his brandy bottle. He couldn't drink another drop. There was an island to get to for rest. Ferris had said the name. Now he should go. Holy cow, he'd better go now. Now, now, now. He was getting high.

He took the next boat. There was no navy to command him and he rested easy without a foreign language tossed at him. The island Ferris had recommended would be enough to confuse him.

Coin stayed alone watching the boat ride into the harbor.

Ferris must have dropped into the sea.

The little boat began to land. Waving the flags of his mirth, there was Ferris, bright, starched, confident, standing on the shore as if he had not left Coin at all with the bottle of brandy and evil sucking all around.

With his ditty bag over his shoulder, Coin went down the gangplank to meet him.

"Boy," said Ferris, "this place is kingdom come. Wait till you see it. Knock your eyes out."

Coin was dazed. The white sun forked down on white, pink, and blue houses. All the colors were innocent. The little boys, begging to carry luggage, seemed already old, beautiful, creased. Eager and dark and knowing, they darted here and there to earn whatever there was to be had. Coin looked up and saw the giant tooth of a volcano mountain piercing the sky, stark as a Jeremiah prayer, gray as his father's hair, loaded with legend.

He followed Ferris to a cafe in the small square of the village. As he sat down a woman, powdered with starch or flour, rushed toward him whispering a strange Italian out of a gargling throat. Coin must have looked amazed because Ferris put his hand on his shoulder.

"Chile, keep yourself together, it's only Consuela and she's the only one. Knows the beginning and the end of everything here. If she don't like you, chile, you might as well dive into the sea."

Consuela stood there, panting. Her hair, parted in the middle, looked as if dyed with black shoe

142

polish, had no luster. Her behind was straight as a palisade. Her hands, spread on her apron, were vises to grip your money or your soul. She was smiling and distant, summing up and down the new visitors.

"Buon giorno," she said to them.

"Va bene," answered Ferris, grinning with insolent composure.

Coin wished he could enjoy himself and be as cool. He was always uncomfortable and scared in new places. He no sooner entered a place but he was ready to run out. The three-hour crossing on the boat had tired him. He still felt the pure sun, hot and foreign on his body. The tropical beauty had been such a swift change. But he felt he would find some secret peace on this island to be his furlough home.

"Wake up, Coin," Ferris nudged. "Boy, this espresso coffee is strong enough for sin to trot on."

Coin looked around the room. It had the peculiar dilapidation acne gives to skin. Someone has pasted magazine covers on the ceiling. Faces stared down on him. He was sitting right under Chiang Kai-shek and the Duke and Duchess of Windsor. Their faces didn't recommend the place. The paint on the walls was peeling in full flakes of white and orange. The chairs jutted from under the tables like dirty fingernails. The espresso machine spit, hissed as Consuela made coffee.

Ferris had turned to the table next to them where a boy sat, looking for all the world like a penguin.

His hair was starched forward and cut in bangs halfway across his forehead. His shirt was white, so were his face and hands; his clothes were black as prophet's moods without prophecy. His feet were bare. His voice was a sharp soprano. He leaned toward them.

"You say your name is Ferris like a boat, or are you called after the wheel? No matter. A strange but rather intriguing name. I once knew a woman by the name of Moon. My aunt, she was in fact. I collect names. She had a daughter called Muh. Whenever I said Aunt Moon, the sun seemed to shine on me. How long will you nice boys be around? I always like to know the dramatis personae of an island." He smoothed his bangs forward with a languid hand covered with freckles.

"I've a passion for islands. I seem to swim from one to the other in the Mediterranean. They call me a penguin because I wear black and white, never get dark in the sun or change my expression. Expression is for oneself and not for others. I loathe doing anything for others. It's loathesome, outward show. Isn't that so, my dear?' and he patted Coin's thigh. "Isn't that truly so. Mmmmm," he turned to Coin directly, "you have the true thing. Saw it as soon as you entered. My name is Bill. Ordinary, isn't it? But the ordinary *can* be spectacular."

Ferris and Horace were grinning but Coin was angry. Jerking away he started for the door and blindly crashed into a girl carrying a basket of flowers. Flowers flew everywhere, splashed in the air, settled soundlessly. No one bothered to look, Coin noticed, so he bent to gather them up. The girl, he knew, was looking at him. He got intensely industrious, finally presenting a filled basket to her. Consuela, who had watched the scene, suddenly yelled out in Italian what must have meant "Get into the kitchen, Fortunata. Quick, quick."

Coin had handed the flower basket to her on his knees. He knelt there watching while she retreated into the dark. For a moment her hands had held the basket toward him. Fortunata. Fortunata was her name. Fortunata!

Meanwhile, Bill was pointing out the local celebrities. He whispered, "There's Paolo the sculptor. Mad as the March wind. When he lived in Milano he was married to an actress with the longest hair in Italy. He heard his wife was having an affair with one of the priests. One day he took her out onto the balcony, seized her by the hair, tossed her over the railing and swung her like a pendulum. You could hear her scream halfway across the city. She left him after that.

"There's May. My enemy. A Midwestern girl. Imagine *that* name for an Amazon. Oh, the bitch! Reported me to the authorities once. I reported her back. One day I'm going to tell that bitch off."

Bill paused to sip his drink as a voice cried out, "My dear, I tell you, it is not to be believed." In the doorway stood a slim man, an older version of the statue of David. Beside him stood a girl with a sweet, sad smile. She looked like a madonna who

145

had lost her halo but was smiling just the same. Inexplicably, Coin felt sorry for her. The man continued, "She really has bras of gold lamé . . .?"

"Oh," screamed Bill as he rushed toward them, "darlings, where have you been? Let me introduce three of the greatest who just arrived. They came on one of those beautiful battleships from America with the entire navy."

Coin couldn't bear Bill as he introduced them with one arm in the air, the pinky bent. "This," announced Bill, "is Horace, this is Ferris, like the wheel, you know," and putting his free arm around Coin, "and this is one with the loveliest name, C-O-I-N, like real American money. Money-boy, here are Franz and Barbara. You are bronze; they are the true silver. My best friends, absolutely my best. I love 'em both. They are hard currency, sailor boys, from Switzerland and the good old U. S. A." He laughed big, artifical ha, ha's. He hugged Franz and Barbara. "Are you the one who wears the bras of gold lamé?" Bill sniggered as he touched her breast. Barbara blushed. Franz disengaged himself and lit a cigarette.

The other patrons focused on them with disgust in their eyes although their mouths laughed. Fortunata had reappeared and hung her head as she watched the scene. Coin wanted to rush over to her, put his arms around her and say that everything would be all right; that he was all right, that she would be all right and that . . . somehow, in some

146

way life wasn't always like this: crowded and hurt and lying and messy.

In his mind was his mother bending over the washtub, scrubbing long underwear, humming about Zion, sweating to keep her family clean. He envisioned Fortunata's mother, with tears of tiredness, caring for Fortunata in the bright sun and breeze of this place. He imagined Fortunata ashamed for him to see the scene before them. Ashamed for him to see this in her country.

At his feet was a flower. He picked it up and handed it to Barbara. In his mind he was really giving it to Fortunata, who was standing still watching him. But Fortunata ran out of the room, her legs in black stockings kicking the air. Coin was confused by her swift exit.

"*Mene, Mene, Tekel, Upharsin,* which translated means 'Thou hast been weighed in the balance and found wanting'," Bill shouted aloud to the room. Then Bill, Franz and Barbara screamed, looking toward May and Paolo. The espresso machine hissed. Coin looked up from the scene into the ceiling. The Duke and Duchess of Windsor smiled down at him.

Chapter Seven

A day later Coin met Franz in the square. Franz suggested that they go swimming. Coin hadn't seen any of the beaches that the island was famous for, so he agreed. Franz told him to wait there, that he'd be back with equipment. Meanwhile, Coin watched the activities in the square. Women passed through with great loads of clothes or piles of grass on their heads. They stood erect and their burdens never wavered. The young men leaned in doorways waiting for something to happen; adolescent girls sauntered in pairs to and fro; sisters of the church, in hats that flew up like wings, herded children about; the mailman delivered letters and packages, stopping to chat or have a drink. A row of trees on either side of the square, the gnarled, thick branches grotesque and strong, sent up foliage lit by the strong sun. They reminded Coin of candelabra twisted by raging fire. The lovely, inventive chanting of children playing games rose up and

149

down in concentrated, disconnected joy. Overhead the sky was contented baby blue. Siesta time. Calm. The square almost deserted.

Franz came running up: eager, smiling, and loaded with diving equipment. "We must run quickly to catch the bus." They scooted off together, ramming themselves into the crowded bus.

The beach was about two miles long with jets of craggy rocks making private pools where one could swim bare-ass because there was a palisade high up behind with no railing. Whoever tried to look down would topple over. They took off their clothes, separately, between the hard secrecy of rocks. Coin left his shorts on. "Coin, take your shorts off, no one will see you. Be free. My God, be free for once." Franz's voice seemed an order and a joy.

Coin was naked in Italy, naked to Italian sun in Mrs. Renaldo's country. When he got home he'd tell her that the blue sky and the aqua sea were like the laughing she and his mother had done together. Sun glinted onto everything, juggling jewels in the air.

"Come on," said Franz, plunging from a rock into the water. Coin followed and they swam out and out, then back into the shelter of the old rocks that had been smoothed for ages into hard rags of sculpture. Coin saw mythological animals in them, with stone-frozen birds perching on their backs. Franz offered him a mask with a stiff tube reaching upward from the nozzle and told him how to adjust the apparatus so that he could stay under to see the flora and fauna. Sunlit golden fish and tribes of sea animals played under the water. Flowers clung to undersea rocks. Fierce yellow sea-blue-green and purple with quavering light everywhere, the flowers and fish lived their fierce, lovely, remote lives. The largest shape before him was the elongated form of Franz. Coin swam up to finish his afternoon, thinking of what he had seen. He lay on the beach with a towel over him. Franz came over. "You must see my birds," he said. "Barbara will have lunch for us."

"Birds?"

"Oh, yes, I must have birds."

Under orange and lemon trees, they sat in the small garden of the villa. Franz had brought out his elaborate cage, set under trees a little distance from the luncheon table. The birds began to sing. Their songs were simple, light, disjointed. The first spring flowers were everywhere. Flowering vines ran up the walls of the villa. The air was sweet with their odor, mixed with the freshness of new grass. Children from the convent across the way hummed drowsy siesta songs.

Coin felt at peace after lunch, looking at his hosts, feeling a part of this island world. The things he had seen and experienced in the last years were not glad ones, but here under this sky, in this air, he hardly believed evil and cruelty existed. Barbara was knitting. She had confided that their first child was coming after five years of trying. Franz began

151

telling Coin about birds, their migration habits, eating habits, of the marvelous ones you could let out of the cage and who always flew back, fluttering at the small wire door, to sleep at home again, resting to enjoy tomorrow's freedom.

"Oh, Barbara, wait until Easter and the Gloria. Shall I tell Coin?"

"Let it be a surprise. On Easter go to the church at nine o'clock sharp because if you don't, you'll miss it."

Coin was bewildered but knew by the expression on their faces that whatever was going to happen would be pleasant. He'd like to ask Fortunata to go with him. But so far he hadn't even talked to her. Not one word.

"Do you suppose Fortunata would go with me?"

"I think so, if you wanted to go with her brother, too," answered Franz.

"I'll ask her," said Coin in a small voice.

"Oh," said Barbara, "they're a wonderful family. They're poor but such fun and devoted to each other. Yes, ask Fortunata, and then you'll meet her brother Ottobre and maybe that'll be a beginning. Once they meet you I'm sure they'll like you."

Coin felt a lump of joy rising within him; he smiled at them. Looking around the garden, he saw nothing had changed because he was changing, but he noticed that the shadows were in different places, that the light seemed to come from within the flowers and the leaves.

Fortunata.

"Have you learned any Italian, Coin?" He shook his head. "You should, it's a beautiful language. Like harpsichord music when it's properly spoken. I remember when I was at home in Ohio there was a church in my neighborhood called Santa Maria della Grazie. Once an Italian who had just come over said the name for me. The words flowed out like music and from that ti. . . ."

"Shhhhhh," whispered Franz fiercely. Barbara and Coin looked in the direction Franz indicated. A dog was slowly crouching, creeping along the garden wall toward the bird cage. Their three heads followed him. Out of one corner of Coin's eye he saw Franz's face become dark and his eyes glinty. Suddenly Franz picked up a stone. With one terrible, accurate throw the stone hit the dog in the temple and blood oozed out thick and hot. The dog was still, his eyes open, dead, staring at the birds. They stopping singing.

"Oh Franz, Franz, Franz," called Barbara, with her hands on her swelling stomach. "I'm going to be sick, take me inside."

Franz stayed crouching on the ground. "That's the dog that killed my birds." The savage look in his eyes scared Coin.

"Franz," continued Barbara, "take me inside. Help me inside. How could you?"

Franz spoke in groans. What he said had more stones in it. He seemed an animal himself. Now he was crying hoarsely, shaking as he put his arm around his wife. Together they wept toward the house.

As Coin approached the garden gate to leave, he noticed that the wet blood had exploded on the white wall and was glistening in the sun.

Since the afternoon with Franz, whenever he was apprehensive or scared or anxious or nervous, Coin rubbed his left arm where his uniform covered the tattoo. The tattoo seemed to burn him. He knew it was merely his imagination but the sensation was there. He could rationalize it but not deny it. Now as he saw Franz, with a bottle under his arm, coming toward him, he ran up a side lane to avoid him and be alone once more with the burning letters on his arm.

Coin passed through a grove of olive trees. He remembered reading somewhere that Milton, when he was old and blind, sometimes held a few olives in his hand to remind him of his golden year in Italy. Coin wondered what he would remember in times ahead about this island where poverty and hard work made the people devout and foreigners seem mad. Just ahead was a space red with poppies bowing and nodding to each other in the sea breeze. They were the sensational red of the blood of martyrs and saints he had seen in pictures in Neapolitan store windows, not the color of the blood of dogs. He rubbed his left arm unconsciously and sat down looking over the sea, thinking.

A shadow covered him. He looked around quickly. Fortunata was behind him, carrying an armful of calla and Easter lilies.

"Buon giorno," she whispered.

"Buon giorno," he answered.

For once he didn't feel foolish or shy. It was as if this meeting had been planned for this time, in this place. Fortunata sat down beside him, placing her flowers between them, and smiled. Then they looked out to sea for a long time. After a while they rose together.

She looked into his eyes gravely. *"Domani a questa ore,* yes?" He watched her moving between the olive trees; the lilies jutting from one arm seemed an angel's wing.

"Domani," he said softly. Yes, tomorrow he would meet her and ask her about Easter.

Fortunata. He would always remember her. He was certain of it.

How long he had dozed among the poppies, he couldn't tell. It must have been a long time. The sky was the pink and white and green of watermelon. The sound of the sea was a cool whisper. He clasped his knees, thinking of the seashell his father had given him long ago. He should have known then that he would hear the same sound again thousands of miles from home at another time. This time.

"Hello, Coin." Coin scratched his left arm. It was Franz. "Do you mind very much if I sit down."

"No," Coin answered. There was nothing else to say.

"Are you angry with me?"

"Why should I be?"

"About the dog, I mean?"

"No. Please leave me alone."

"I saw you turn up the lane this afternoon so you would not have to say hello. Is hello much to say to a friend? Hello, Coin."

"Hello, Franz."

"Thank you."

Coin couldn't say any more. He didn't feel uneasy anymore. *"Domani a questo ore,"* she had said. He was waiting for that.

"I must make a confession, Coin. I followed you here. I followed you here and I am ashamed of myself. Do you forgive me? Please."

"Yes. Did you hear what she said?"

Franz sighed with satisfaction. "I heard but don't be afraid. I won't tell."

Now Coin could not come here tomorrow, and Fortunata would be waiting with her flowers. If he came Franz would be watching, even if he didn't tell anyone.

"It is," said Franz, "a secret between us."

"Don't make it so mysterious; there's no secret nothing. I haven't done anything and you're just a busybody. Please, Franz, leave me alone."

"All right." But he sat still. They watched the sun drop down into the Tyrrhenian Sea. After a while Franz began to whistle "Santa Lucia," softly, like an echo in a bell.

"How's Barbara?" asked Coin.

"Barbara? She's gone to Naples to shop." He continued to whistle "Santa Lucia," finished the song. "Do you know who Santa Lucia was?"

"No, I don't. We used to sing about her in school, that's all I know, besides. . . ."

Franz continued, "She was a lovely girl. Lovelier even than Barbara. Her eyes made men tongue-tied with love and they threw themselves into the sea, in grief, because she would not love them. They came from all over Italy to kill themselves for one look from her. They were possessed."

Coin was fascinated, and sat upright like a boy in the fifth grade.

"One day a king came to court her. When he was led into her room, she stood up and looked at him. Her eyes touched him beyond his heart into his soul. They were flower eyes as well as prophecy eyes, Mary's eyes. He spread gifts before her of gold and all the world. It was useless. The king moaned in his heart."

Franz lifted the bottle Coin had seen earlier and drank from it.

"Coin, you want some brandy?"

"No."

"Well, I want some brandy and here it it." Franz laughed and was still, holding his offering to Coin in a satyr gesture to fall among the red poppies. "In Lucia's heart there was only one lover, God. The king was an urgent man. He offered to marry her at once, after he had looked into her eyes. Although Lucia wished to be a queen, she almost cried that this king was not the King of Heaven. He was divine. But not *The* Divine . . . you follow me, Coin?"

Franz' head almost fell into Coin's lap.

"I follow you, Franz."

"The king told her how he loved her eyes. He told her he was a very great king. But before her he felt very lowly. 'Oh king,' she said, 'here are my eyes!' She plucked them out and laid them on a silver salver for love of him. Do you know what?"

Coin answered, thinking of Fortunata, "What, Franz?"

"She said, 'I love thee, O king, but I love my God much more'! He left with sorrow in his heart. She rested seventeen days in blindness. The country became foggy and dark. At the end of that time, the sun came out over all of Italy. God had regarded the love this girl had for Him and her eyes grew back."

It was almost dark now. The voice of Franz had hopes and prayers in it.

"You should see the celebration for Santa Lucia," said Franz. "It has passed by my house for seven years. The first year Barbara woke me up to see it. We went out on the balcony. The streets were filled with men and women chanting adoration to Santa Lucia. The women were in black and had shawls on their heads and carried lighted candles.

On the mountain there were fires, flares erupted. A statue of Santa Lucia was being carried on the shoulders of four men. Blood streamed from the eyes: martyr's blood: hard, black, reconciled, finished; in her hand was a plate with her eyes made of jewels. Song . . . mad songs at dawn in a strange language . . . monotone, pagan songs to a Christian saint. This is what I saw."

They were both silent. Franz finally said, "An Italian boy told me the story, and when he finished I must have looked puzzled so he added, 'It's true, too.'" He laughed softly.

"Do you believe it?" asked Coin.

"Believe it? Of course I believe it. Miracles are the only things I think are real." His voice had become intimate. He put his arm around Coin and his hand rested on the tattoo. Coin expected to feel the burning but he didn't. He was thinking of . . . of Santa Lucia and Fortunata, of his mother. The sky was entirely green now and the first star had appeared. He was on Berriman Street, a child again, closed within the seashell of his dreams, listening to the children on his block chant together:

Star light, star bright,
The first star I see tonight,
I wish I may, I wish I might,
Have the wish I wish tonight.

His brother Woody always broke that up by yelling at the top of his lungs:

159

Ladybug, Ladybug,
Fly away home,
Your house is on fire;
Your children are burning. . . .

Franz kissed him on the mouth. The scar burned. He was burning. Fortunata and his mother were burning. He could not bear it. Swiftly he leaped up; without looking at Franz or at anything, he began to run. He ran and ran and ran until he reached the square. All of it was a dream. The whole afternoon. Had Fortunata *or* Franz kissed him? He walked rapidly toward his *pensione.*

The next afternoon he was back in the field of poppies. Fortunata came through the olive trees bearing her flowers. Coin took her in his arms. The flowers were crushed between them, sending out Easter perfume. Then they sat, as they had yesterday, and looked at the sea and at each other. The rustling in the olive grove didn't bother Coin. He knew it was Franz but he knew that this watching and looking with Fortunata was right and good. There was no need to alarm her. He would not run away.

"*A la pasqua, andiamo col mio fratello Ottobre, a la chiesa per guardare la Gloria.*"

Coin pieced the words out. He didn't have to ask her after all.

"*Doppo, andremo a la casa mia per pranzare.* Yes?"

"Yes," answered Coin. Fortunata vanished again through the olive grove.

He would see the Easter Gloria with Fortunata.

Coin and Ferris were sitting in Consuela's. Even in the Zion of his need to tell his friend what was on his mind about Franz and Fortunata, Coin kept silent, scratching his arm. He would have dashed his future children on the stones by the river of Babylon to be able to tell all. But he kept silent. Ferris wouldn't understand or if he did, would laugh, whoop, holler at his innocence. Instead they talked about what they would wear at Bill's masquerade party. Ferris was full of ideas.

"You," Ferris said, "will be a Chinese coolie. We'll make a hat and twist your navy blues. Bare feet and chest." Coin didn't care what he was, Fortunata would not be there.

"I don't know what I'll be. Maybe God's left-hand angel, Lucifer!" He laughed so hard Coin joined in. ". . . or the Belle of St. Mary's!" They roared louder. ". . . maybe I'll wear nothing but painted tattoos." They both shut up at that. "They tell me that Bill's coming as a hermaphrodite and Franz and Barbara will be Romeo and Juliet! That will be the day, with her stomach pushed out! They'd better pull themselves together. Romeo and Juliet! All they have in common is the tomb."

Consuela, Coin noticed, was watching them, probably wondering what the conversation was about, probably knew.

161

As they finished their drinks, Ferris said, "I left my money at the *pensione*. You pay up, Coin." Coin paid.

Outside, Ferris was in the talking mood. "Did I ever tell you about what I did to the lieutenant who riled me at Great Lakes in Chicago? Well, that's one for the classic books. He tried to boot my ass out of ship's company. I booted him into the grave, chile. Indeed I did. It was turkeys did it. I turkey'd him till there was no more help to scream for. On my first furlough I began sending him pictures. One a day. Boy, I worked at it. Then I'd call, he'd answer and I'd say, 'Gobble, gobble, gobble' and hang up."

"You didn't do that, Ferris."

"I sure did. Then I commenced to send him stamps from Turkey. That must have bugged him. Spent a third of my money buying turkeys. Send them to him by special messenger. His wife was probably making dressing all day, every day. I cut out pictures of turkeys and mounted them real nice and sent them. Do you know what I did then?"

"No."

"Chile, I had a turkey telegram sent each night at different times. The voice on the phone would sing out:

Turkey is a hen,
Turkey in the rye;
I gobble you,
You gobble I.

162

"He finally had his telephone cut off. So day after day I'd send him a part of a turkey. A wing, a gizzard, a thigh, a breast. By the time they reached him they must have been rotten.

"After that time I started on feathers. Sent his wife a hat made of turkey feathers. They must'uv died. Sent a quill pen of feathers. Began on his office. Gobble, gobble, gobble, I'd call. And he'd hang up crazy mad. Finally, I sent a live turkey, crated, to the office where he worked. Feller I knew there said he pitched a bitch. They carried him to the veterans' hospital after that. And he's still there, chile, dreaming, I expect, of turkey heaven. I liked to died when I heard the final outcome. In the camp he come asking me about something or other and I asked him, 'Where's my crow'? He said, 'You mean your JIM CROW'. That was the end of him, boy. He's probably hollering 'gobble, gobble, gobble' at this minute and wondering what in the world happened to him." Ferris snickered. "I happened to him. There now!"

Ferris was a Miss Lucy Horwitz cutting at a world.

"He's stark, raving crazy at this minute." Ferris gargled his laugh, ran in circles, then scooted away.

Coin shouted in the direction Ferris ran, "What kind of clown do you think you are, anyhow? I hope you die, Ferris, I hope you swallow your tongue. Go to hell, you crazy lunatic. I never want to see you again. Never!"

163

The party was held in a vast and remote villa where Bill was staying. Ferris, a bright fallen angel of the Lord, and Coin, a dark coolie, arrived in a nightmare rain. In the vestibule shelter of the villa they repaired their damaged costumes. Ferris's wings sloped downward and Coin's hat was a mess. They both flapped and pulled until they were presentable. Then they went upstairs where the laughing company was trying to outdo the noise of the rain. Bill, at the door, was roaring drunk and giggling *"Mene, Mene, Tekel, Upharsin"* to each incomer. His hands were alive with pats. Like one deacon in the Corinthian Baptist Church, he felt up everyone, laying the ground for after the shindig.

"La do da dee, here's my penny, my penny, and my Ferris wheel," he screamed.

Ferris whispered to Coin, "Pay him to mind, chile, his cups have been full and now run over."

Bill was at them again as they entered a large room with balloons hanging from the ceiling and streamers of confetti leading the air at every which turn. "Look," announced Bill, "here are my colored brethren. Now the party can begin." He put his arms about Coin and Ferris. "Here are my lovely chocolate drops of joy."

Ferris pulled away swiftly. "I ain't no chocolate drop of joy or anything, you drunken bastard," and punched Bill in the mouth. Bill staggered back with a weak grin. "La dee da da," Bill said, "I'm not hurt, but I'm mad at you and at you." He pointed at Ferris and then toward Coin and switched away to join the grinning guests.

"Somebody, somebody," he cried, "rescue my eye with a beefsteak or call the police. Police, police, police!"

Bill raised his hand with a cigarette in it. He began to pop the balloons: red, blue, white, purple, green, they shred ragged on high, exhausted of air. With his last leap, he fell to the floor. The guests snickered.

"Coin," said Ferris, "let's get out of here. I'm glad Horace had a headache and refused to come. He would have been out of his mind."

Bill sprang up as they started to go. "No, no, no. You are the chiefest guests, that's from *Hamlet,* oh Lord, no, from *Macbeth,* of course. Scatter, children, scatter, life can be beautiful, lovely, lovely, and beautiful." He shooed the guests to the bar like an eagle chasing swallows. Franz, his eyes bloodshot, walked up to Bill.

"Bill," he said, "Bill, this is enough, calm down."

"Calm down," screamed Bill, "I'll calm down when the moon churns green cheese. You and her," pointing viciously at Barbara, "with her Italian baby growing inside her like a threepenny opera, you both calm down. I ain't gonna calm down. This is my house and you're in it. Now stay—or go. But before you do . . . have another drink, kiddo. My kiddo."

He put his arms around Franz. "Did I make a scene? Yes, I made a scene."

Everyone stood silent in their colorful, long-prepared costumes. Coin watched his time coming as Bill lurched toward him.

"Coin, Coin," he yelled. "Coin doesn't love me. Did you ever love Franz, did you?"

Coin wrapped himself in coolie silence, he wasn't going to utter a thing. He had expected a word from Ferris, who knew how to handle these things, but Ferris kept out. Bill wound up again. "And do you know what I've found out? Ferris is a shit. A shit heel. And," he said, pointing his full arm at everybody, "I despise me." His eyes rolled upward. "Coin," he said, "bring me some gin. You're a colored boy and very, very young, fetch me some gin. You're the only one who will help me, the only one."

Coin turned away. Franz was before him. Barbara behind her husband had tears in her eyes. "Coin," Franz asked, "would you be good to me, too?" Barbara looked to Coin, beseeching behind her husband's back. Say yes, she signaled, say yes. Her hands were holding her stomach. As Coin nodded to Franz, he noticed that Bill had passed out completely on the floor; Ferris was grinning down at him. All the others had begun drinking again. Barbara was in a corner, wounded and humiliated. Coin thought of the dog Franz had killed; now in his drunkenness he was trying to kill an unborn child. He had to leave this house and find Fortunata. Maybe she would be outside waiting for him. Coin walked toward the door. Ferris came swiftly after him.

"Where are you going, kiddo?"

"Out, anyplace away from here."

"Stick around, the fun is about to begin."

Fun! thought Coin. Was this really fun? It was a cesspool. And tomorrow the cussings out, the bruised eyes, the popped balloons, the frustrations, the yapping and yelling would all be forgotten in one enormous hangover.

Ferris took Coin's coolie hat. "You'd better stay here, kiddo, and learn something. You're always running away."

"Look, Ferris," said Coin, "I want something better than this."

"You're a snob, boy. You better look at people and listen; then you'll know what's happening. What are you afraid of, anyhow?"

"I don't want them putting their hands on me." Coin was trembling. "Listen, I'm going now. I'll see you tomorrow." As he started to leave there came a long, piercing scream. They both looked around. Bill had revived and was sitting cross-legged on the floor with May opposite him. They were having a screaming contest. Bill had a piece of meat against his eye. First he would scream at May: AhAhAhAhhhhhhhh. And then May would scream back: Ahahahahahahhhhhhhhhhhhhh.

Laughter shook the room.

Coin turned to Ferris again. "I can see what's

happening and I don't like it." He looked toward Barbara, who was staring first at him, then at Franz. Coin couldn't bear it and ran out of the room, down the steps. He opened the great doors and Fortunata was there. Her eyes invited him to sorrow and joy and a light of constellations of love he never thought he'd know. Drenched by the rain, they ran toward the field of poppies.

Next day the church bells didn't ring out the hours. The church doors were bolted and great spikes had been driven into them. Holy Saturday. Christ had not yet risen. All the women wore black.

Easter Saturday morning Coin got up early for the Gloria. He dressed in his whites and decided to take a walk before meeting Fortunata and her brother. He was scared about meeting her family. But he would go. He had to see what their house was like. Not the house itself. That was unimportant. Was it a bent house like his had been? Or did it hold the courage and strength he sensed in Fortunata? A house his mother might have lived in with joy? A house with good love? A house where there were real holidays? A house without cruel frustrations? A place where time went by and you knew what was going to happen next? He wanted a house that might be a little bit dull with tradition but leisurely in action. He wanted a shape of living to remember and pattern his life by. Oh, he felt alone in the winding sheet of his thoughts!

He began to gather flat stones to skip into the

calm morning sea. One by one he threw them out, making bets with himself. How many skips will this stone make? Three or four or seven? How many skips will I make? Fortunata should be here. He tensed before he threw a tenth stone out, betting: if it skips eight, it will be a good house and they will like him in it. The flat stone skipped eight. Sitting down on a flat rock, he made a vague sign of the cross, played with the sand. When he found a dried starfish, he put it in his upper pocket for luck, for Fortunata, for hope.

Standing outside the church, he saw them moving toward him, hand in hand. Her great, earnest eyes reached him even from a distance. They sent messages of the night before—lighthouse signals to the distressed, to those in trouble, those in love. Before he could remember what color her eyes were, she was there with her brother Ottobre, somber and richly dark, southern Italian and real. Her eyes were no color; all colors; mostly gold flecks breaking through blue, brown. They were a shrine. He wanted to bow before them. Instead he said *"Buon giorno"* to both of them and the three solemnly entered the ornate, humble church these people of God had prepared with love for His Son and for mankind.

There was confusion everywhere. Cats and dogs licked and smelled, running about with the careless, knowing darts of animals. Babies cried in the confusion of the scene. Women in Bible black, unconcerned with animals, held premeditated seances with the Mother of Christ, a silent lip-moving particular to this moment of celebration when the Savior will rise again in glory. They prayed His mother Mary, in grief, to send a benediction to their lives of poverty, and send, in turn, their men to sea for a blessed harvest.

Before the great altar there was a blue curtain with hundreds of silver stars. Men were pulling at it to make sure it would fall right. Coin could see acolytes lighting candles behind the altar. Presently, from where he sat with Fortunata and Ottobre, he could see the church was in order. Chairs were straight, animals were gone. A little bell began to ring, a stronger bell sounded, then the clang of the tower bells, then bells over the town sounded. They were harsh, iron, sincere, loud, bells of the poor.

"Gloria," whispered Fortunata.

Suddenly, from the cornices of the church, confetti of every color fell down softly like rain. Then doves in joyous freedom flew through the bright paper. The children sang the word "HALLELUJAH" over and over again. "HALLELUJAH, HALLE-LUJAH, HALLELUJAH, HALLELUJAH." The curtain before Mary's altar fell down. Everyone sang "HALLELUJAH." There seemed to be a million candles and lilies and flowers of all descriptions. Everybody kneeled. Christ was flying up to God. Mary in infinite compassion stayed with the people. Her face was lonely, afraid and exultant. These people had made this statue to her love and they were here with longing eyes to beg peace.

HALLELUJAH. The doves whirled everywhere. The Gloria was finished. Their HALLELUJAH sounded pagan and terrible and right to Coin. Fortunata and her brother were looking at him. He was in their country at last.

After the service he walked to their house along a road with walls of porous green rock on each side. The walls went up in tiers on the mountainside, holding the earth back. Every scrap of land was cultivated. There were olive trees, fig trees, lemon and orange trees, grape vines, gardens where squash grew, and onions, lettuce, tomatoes, and whatnot! The breeze from the sea set all the leaves to fluttering, designing the air. Far up on the mountain there were pines here and there, gnarled by wind and weather, but enduring. Their umbrella-shaped heads had refused to bow down. The sea glittered with the sun on it. Donkeys passed along making loud, cracking sounds protesting against their beast-burdened lives. Sometimes people ran out onto their balconies to see the dark man in white. They called to Fortunata and Ottobre, pointed to Coin, smiling friendship and curiosity. Coin smiled back.

"Buon giorno," they cried.

"Buon giorno," the three of them waved back. He felt happy and light. Ottobre pointed to a house high in a near hill. *"Quello e noi casa."*

It was a rambling house made of the same porous rock of the walls, commanding a view of the

171

sea; Capri rode camellike on the sea in the distance.

Instead of going to the house at once, Fortunata led him to a lookout. A beach was below. The sand sparkled like millions of Fourth of July sparkles. The sea had made coves everywhere. The shapes of the rocks were animals, birds, flowers, stars, the shapes of good and bad dreams. When they finally entered the house, Ottobre introduced him.

"Mama, Papa, Anna . . . Coin."

They all smiled at him. Then two children came toward him. Inspecting him. Coin patted them. They ran away giggling. Anna rushed after them. Everybody burst out laughing. The laughter made Coin feel at home, so he joined in. Before he knew it a glass of wine was in his hand and he began to talk. No one understood, of course, but they all listened and talked back. He was reminded in a flash of the conversations his mother had had with Mrs. Renaldo. It didn't matter what they said. They understood each other through the eyes and the heart. This is what Coin felt now, realizing that Fortunata's family felt the same way.

Mama was Fortunata forty years from now; one of those pines he had seen along the way. Her legs were spread apart under a burlap skirt. She fanned a face that had been slapped around by the weather and creased with work. She looked like she had crossed the river of Jordan time after time and fought her way back, because she was the center of those about her now. She knew Mary would receive her when she was ready to come, but she would leave forever only in her own good time. Now Papa was playing a wonderful, sad guitar, singing Neapolitan songs like kingdom come. The whole family, including the children who had returned, joined the choruses. They drowned out the sea. Presently Mama left to fix dinner. Papa passed around more wine and sang more songs.

The house looked like it had grown up out of the earth. Inside there was sturdy, simple furniture. The table was spread for the Easter meal. Even though Coin couldn't understand what the family said, their gestures were large, expressive, emotional. Often one of them broke out into song like a lyrical eruption. He felt the warmth and sincerity of their living. Only Fortunata was a little grave as she cast him looks of longing that he knew would someday break his heart when he remembered them. She knew he had to leave tomorrow. They both wanted to memorize their hours together against what might be empty, dry times ahead.

The children showed Coin their pathetic, homemade toys, glowing with affection for them.

Fortunata showed him family pictures: Mama and Papa after their wedding standing formal and frightened, looking out to their future now; Fortunata in her white confirmation veil; Ottobre in his first long pants; the sister Anna with her children at the beach; her husband, cuddling the boy and girl smiling up at him, rare bird-singing smiles. Coin saw the scrapbook of their lives together and he loved them and what they were like: the simplicity of water with the strength of homemade bread.

After dinner they took him round to little cafes by the sea and drank white wine with their friends, who welcomed him by clicking their glasses with his. At the last cafe someone played an accordion against the sound of the waves. Night came on slowly as if ashamed to cover all that had shone on his last day. Nearing the house again, the family walked ahead. Coin and Fortunanta were just behind. Coin fetched the dried starfish from his pocket and put it into her hand.

"Grazie," she said.

Now they were at the house, all of them. Papa leaped up on a low wall and sang a parting song to Coin. The family joined the chorus. Then, as they stood in a semicircle around him, he shook Papa's and Ottobre's hands. Ottobre looked deep into his eyes. He kissed the little boy and the little girl. When he got to Mama she opened her strong arms and enfolded him. Then looking at Fortunata, she whispered *"Ritorno."*

As he went down the road he heard their calls, *"Arriverderci, arriverderci, arriverderci."* He could have bowed down his head and cried. Cried for so much goodness around him, so much love. Suddenly he wiped his eyes and laughed the last *arriverderci.*

Arriverderci!

Chapter Eight

Coin was thinking about sin as the little boat crossed the Tyrrhenian Sea to Naples. From there he would be sailing to Brooklyn again, leaving some magic behind, holding some within himself, he knew, forever. Sitting by himself in a sheltered corner on the middle deck, he brooded hard and long. He sacrificed his last chance to look at the glories of the waters, mountains, houses he was passing, on the altar of his thoughts where all the candles were dead. The shape and smell and color of sin was the shape and color and smell of his mind—the actions he had witnessed days, years ago. He wanted to know how and why he had committed a fearful and wonderful joy with Fortunata, lying on red poppies in a tempest of tropical rain. That sin was black and beautiful, performed near the edges of danger. Suppose Mary-hearted Fortunata should have a child when he wasn't close to defend her or claim his own? Her family's shame would rise up to make him sleepless. How they had loved and trusted him in one afternoon ... remembering it made him once more want to bow down his head and not cry, but weep. He thought of Ottobre's eyes when he bade him farewell, good-bye. He wondered if the brother knew about the red sin gathered in the flowers, in furious, needle rain. Oh, that sharp water had washed away loneliness, prepared for happiness and flooded it away. His sin in taking Fortunata was a necessary and vital disaster; warm, cold, right and as real as lire to Neapolitans or the hard blood of the saints to God.

He thought of the procession on the island, dedicated to Maria Dolorosa: Mary in sorrow on Good Friday carried on the shoulders of four men, her figure draped in black. Children pelted her with flowers. The crowds in the streets wept for their lives. Coin dug for a meaning. This Mary, high up on mortal shoulders, had known sin. He wondered if the love of God had been sweet. But her act had been with God and for the eternal salvation of man.

Sin again. The only beloved Son of Mary and God had committed the sin of martyrdom because He realized that His Father wanted to wrest the world from sin. Coin visioned Mary, snapping butterbeans within the shadows of terrible, crucifying Golgotha, waiting for Him to come home. What did she care about the treaties of kings? What did she care about wars except that the men were there and should be elsewhere: in Bethlehem, perhaps, or

176

Brooklyn or Sacramento or Mesopotamia, lighting family fires?

Fortunata was looking now at the sea because he had looked at it. He felt that the colors had changed for her because she had looked at it *with* him. Without Fortunata he felt isolated. He put his head against the back of the bench, gazed upward where birds were making crazy designs in the sky and whispered, "Mother, come get me, I've got poppies in my hand." It may have been Naomi Starr Foreman he was addressing, or Mary, the conceiver of Christ.

He was on his way to Brooklyn to no house, to no house. The concrete meaning of his life was in his ditty bag: the seashell, yes, the seashell. The boat lurched and he was on the deck. He crawled toward his fallen ditty bag. When he had reached it and the boat settled to normal he opened it to find the other important thing he kept with him. It was a book of autographs his teachers and classmates had signed when he graduated from high school. Here it was: the imitation cushioned leather cover, the gilt edges, the pages of different colors. He opened his past and the waves of his mind parted to let it through. He read, *To Coin: Don't suck lollypops: SUC-CESS, from your Bro.-grad-u-8— Teddie Esterbrook.* On a blue-green page was the message: *To Coin, It is by chance that we are brothers but hearts that make us friends, Your brother, Woody Foreman,* and at the four corners of the paper were printed *For Get Me Not* (the corners were full of home). He turned to a pink page: *To Coin, Here's to the years that are stretching ahead, The days that are blithesome and gay. May the joys of the old year be the joys of the new and the sorrows fade away. Your sis-ter grad-u-8, Esther*. Esther. What had happened to her? Another one: *Coin, Being no Poet, possessing no fame Permit me just to sign my name. Your brother grad-u-8, Abie Fox.*

Then he read Agnes's message on a pure-white page: *Deep in the heart of each living soul lies the hidden dream of a perfect life*. On a yellow page: *To Coin, Be brave, strong and hearty, never be the color of this page. Your loving sister, Bernice*. He sat very still. He couldn't think anything out, not now, not now. He saw the U.S.S. *Commodore* waiting to take him back to the streets where he played marbles when he was a boy, to take him past the house chocked full with ghosts and anger and . . . and Agnes's hidden dream of a perfect life. (Miss Lucy had had iron bars put on all the windows after Agnes died; she had jailed herself in.)

Then he saw Lieutenant Commander Mark approaching; he became a sailor again. Stood up and saluted smartly. Lieutenant Commander Mark was from Alabama but he had chosen Coin to be his yeoman. They had gotten on well together. Lieutenant Commander Mark liked books and sometimes after hours asked Coin into his cabin, where they spent an hour or two reading aloud to each

178

other. He told Coin about his family and showed him pictures of them. He seemed like the kind of man Coin's father might have been when he was young. And he smoked a vicious cigar. In the small cabin that sharp smoke hit the nose as well as the ceiling, and sometimes Coin saw the pockmarked commander only through the hot fog of the smoke. But they got Tennyson together and Keats, Milton, and the Brontes. Other times Lieutenant Commander Mark just talked between reading. Coin remembered once (when the commander was obviously drunk) that he had read a poem by Emily Bronte; one stanza came back:

Oh dreadful is the check, intense the agony—
When the ear begins to hear, and the eye begins
    to see;
When the pulse begins to throb—the brain to
    think again—
The soul to feel the flesh, and the flesh to feel the
    chain.

The verse seemed to fill Coin's life with startles of meaning.

Suddenly the officer had asked for his teeth. He said he had lost them, misplaced them, hidden them. They both went on their hands and knees looking for the loot of the commander's mouth. When Coin found a box where the commander kept his watch and World War I medals, he lifted the lid and saw two pictures, one of a Negro boy and one of a Negro girl who looked just like his officer.

The U.S.S. *Commodore* was preparing to sail. Coin hadn't seen Ferris since he left the island and he was curious and wondering. The next day was sailing time and still no Ferris.

When the U.S.S. *Commodore* began to churn away, Coin gave Ferris up. The boy was probably with Horace in Naples. He didn't care for regulations or about Coin. Probably in Naples getting additional tattoos or wrestling in the bars of the Galleria Umberto. True to form Ferris arrived in a tender with Horace grinning his seaweed smile, two hours after the *Commodore* had set to sea. It took a long time for the ship to halt, but it halted and Ferris and Horace climbed aboard. Lieutenant Commander Mark walked by Coin, tending to business at his desk, and went into his office without speaking. Coin sensed a crisis at hand. It wouldn't be an ordinary one.

Soon the Atlantic churned under the hull of the island-of-a-ship. Land had become merely a memory. The lights of Italy and time had gone out. Total isolation began.

The commander came out of his office and spoke to Coin.

"Seaman First Class Ferris Wing and Seaman First Class Horace Jones will report here. Let them in at once." He was abrupt and sharp in command. The door hit shut. The churn, churn, churn of the sea carried on. Coin waited, while he typed routine reports, for his friends' final judgment. It didn't take long. Ferris and Horace approached his desk like a laugh. Even the positions of their bodies seemed to say ha ha, ha ha ha. But Ferris had no-kidding in his voice when he asked Coin if he could see Lieutenant Commander Mark at once.

Coin rapped on the door smartly, opened it and announced, "Seaman First Class Ferris Wing and Seaman First Class Horace Jones are present to see you, sir." The lieutenant commander nodded yes and the sailors went into the office. Coin was so excited he forgot to close the door. The other yeomen were typing slowly, carefully. Coin returned to his desk to sort clips, untangle rubber bands, shuffle papers, change the calendar to next month, load the stapling machine, examine the insignia sewed to his blouse. Underneath his yeoman's crow, his arm began to itch. The letters of his tattoo began to crawl under his uniform. Inside the commander's office he caught a glimpse of Ferris and Horace, erect, correct, and between their bodies the face of the navy working in navy talk. The words issued out: precise, earnest, sincere, official. All the other yeomen's typewriters had stopped. The voice of the navy swept forth.

"You will be confined to your quarters until the end of this trip. At which time you will be subject to further discipline. That is all."

Ferris's words hit Coin, the neutral walls of the

office, spit into the sea, turned the faces of the other yeomen beet-red.

"I'll tell the captain, I'll tell the captain. Don't you ever call me nigger again. Don't you call me that again, or Horace. You hear me?" Ferris was retreating from the room with a finger pointing in acting-out wrath.

The lieutenant commander followed his accusing finger, saying quietly, "I never said that, I never called one of my men out of his name."

But Ferris had run out and so had Horace. The officer said his last words to nothing. When he turned around he looked at Coin long, hard, and lasting. Typewriters began going again. As he moved toward the open door to his office, he said, "I don't think there is anything more today." Then his voice got solid and full of Alabama and navy. "I don't think I'll need you again today, Seaman . . . Yeoman First Class Foreman." Then he strode into his sanctuary and locked the door.

Coin walked slowly to his bunk. He held to the desk trying not to vomit. He wanted the Atlantic to wash Ferris into the stomach of its waters. The worst thing was that he wanted sharks for his friend. As he groped into his bunk he murmured:

"I hope you die and go to hell soon, Ferris . . . soon."

Coin didn't sleep much. All night long he wanted to get to Lieutenant Commander Mark and talk to him; he didn't know just what he'd say. He did know that there would be no more wonderful reading sessions, that he'd lost one of the best friends he'd ever have. He had to see Ferris by hook or by crook and have the whole thing out with him. He hoped he hadn't cried or talked in his sleep.

In the morning no one looked at him strangely so he guessed he had acted all right. After a spoonful of chow he decided to go to the library and get a load of books and daze himself by reading; although by now he had read almost all of the books it seemed. He knew the shelves almost by heart. Coin dreaded meeting the commander in the morning light. He couldn't face those sleepless eyes now. And so he took a devious route to the deck where the library was. He felt like Raskolnikov eluding Police Inspector Porfiry. He felt guilty as if by having been Ferris's friend before, he had betrayed his commander. Deep down, too, he felt color guilt, race guilt. And yet there was no need, none at all. But the feeling concentrated in the tattoo on his arm, the itch there would not stop no matter how much he rubbed and fretted. Once, while he was moving along, treading the soft-boiled eggs of his conscience, he thought he heard the commander's voice giving orders. Sweat broke out under his arms and he looked around for a place to hide. Then he remembered that Marky—that's what the sailors called him privately—was in a big conference with the other officers. They held it every week at this time. He wondered if the subject of Ferris and

Horace had been brought up. But anyway, everyone must know about it by now.

He moved against a bulkhead, thinking foolishly that he could hide himself (and the incident) in the sunlight. The voices trailed away. After a moment he walked on cautiously; the pounding he heard was not the engines but his heart. A plan was taking shape in his mind but for the life of him he couldn't tell what it was; the juices were there though and, if he didn't think, they would mix right. The library should be open by now, and he approached it with almost a swagger. Charlie, the ship's librarian, was sitting at his desk sorting some books as Coin entered.

"Hi there," said Charlie with hearty, morning cheer, "you're in early."

"Oh, I've got a few hours to kill. Too early?"

"Nope. Come on in. We've got a whole load of new books, picked them up from the sea mail this morning about three A.M. Even some you haven't read before." He laughed and Coin felt better. "Say, Coin, will you hold it down for me for a sec or so, I've got to go to the head and you know all the merchandise in case anyone comes in."

"Sure, sure."

When Charlie left he looked around at his friends on the walls. They were permanent. Everlasting, evermores. They would be somewhere in the world if the ship went down to the ocean bottom. These weren't the only ones; there were copies in many languages. But there was only one Ferris, one Lieutenant Commander Mark, one Fortunata, one Franz, one Bernice, and one, only one of all those he had met and loved. He didn't feel like living inside a book with lovers and friends. He wanted them created in life and he wanted his friends to create him.

Well, he would do the best he could. Without being truly conscious of it he began softly to repeat to himself:

Oh dreadful is the check, intense the agony—
When the ears begin to hear, and the eyes begin
    to see;
When the pulse begins to throb—the brain to
    think again—
The soul to feel. . . .

Something was behind him; there was no shadow or sound; a fear waiting at his back. He refused to turn. If he turned he knew he would do something he shouldn't do, something disgraceful, with shame in it. He rasped through his teeth, "Ferris, go away, get out of here, get."

"Oh, come on, boy, don't act like that, we're too old friends for you to act like that. I didn't mean anything . . . I was. . . ." Coin felt the hand on his shoulder and he clasped both fists.

"Take your hands off me; I'm trying to count to ten, Ferris . . . don't make me do it. Take off that fucking hand."

"You ain't a good fighter, Coin, you're a soft fighter."

Mad as he was, Coin heard the soft chuckle. As he ripped around, Ferris was still repeating, "You're a soft fighter, Coin, a soft, soft fighter." Ferris had a hunter's grip on his face and hard pebbles in his eyes. "What kind of a colored guy are you, taking up for that poor white trash. Listen, boy, if you don't find some way to get me out of this, I'll whip your ass from here to Montezuma and then some."

Coin's blood hit him in every pulse. He raised one arm and hit Ferris so that he lay across a table, bent backwards. When he began to stir, Coin was standing over him to let him have it again and again. Ferris opened first one eye and then the other. He folded up, sitting on the table, and nursing his cheek said, "Boy, you've got a battleship left. Didn't know you had a battleship left." He started walking a few feet toward the door. Coin was still panting, amazed and glad at what had happened. Ferris took a step toward him with an outstretched hand and a grin Coin had never seen before.

"I told you to get out," Coin said.

"All right, all right, murder boy." Ferris started toward the door, but from a table he swiftly picked up a giant Webster's dictionary and, running toward Coin, smashed it on his head. Then he picked up another book and threw it at Coin as he was recovering from the dictionary blow. The fight was on. Coin knew that this was the beginning or the end of him. He backed toward a bookcase and hurled Spinoza at Ferris and whammed him in the eye. A book came at him like a fat, accurate arrow and he ducked. Novels, history, geography, astronomy, philosophy whirled across the room. Jane Austen smacked Kipling in the middle of the air. Shakespeare landed on Ferris as he bent to pick up *Moby Dick*. *A Shropshire Lad* hit Coin near his Adam's apple, naval history landed on tables. Ferris cursed as he hit or missed, Coin crying out loud as he threw his friends and knowledge across the room. Then someone pinned back his arms and across the room he saw Ferris pinned back, too, jerking forward for release. Behind the main table stood Lieutenant Commander Mark. Sailors clustered in the doorway. Silence screamed everywhere. The commander looked at the sailors, eyed Charlie, and Charlie cleared the room. The commander sat down behind the table, Coin panting in one corner and Ferris in another rubbing one shoe on his pants and then the other to polish them. It was crazy.

The commander's voice started evenly like a plane sharpening tough wood. "Wing," he began as he looked at the polishing motion, "I don't think you need polished shoes in the brig. First, you have insulted a naval officer, secondly, you escaped from your quarters; you have been insolent, you're AWOL, you're a troublemaker, no mistake. All in all you're a disgrace to your friend here and probably to everyone who ever came in contact with you." Coin hearing the irony in the way Marky used "friend," sensed that everything wasn't all lost for him.

Ferris didn't bother to look at either of them. But when the commander said, "You'll be facing a court-martial, Wing," Ferris looked rapidly twice from the commander to Coin. It was the only emotion Coin saw him show. "A court-martial!" the commander went on. "There will be enough witnesses. I'm . . . I'm only sorry you're colored. I wish I didn't have to make an exhibition of that." He moved rapidly to the door and Coin heard him ask Charlie to send in the officer of the deck.

After Ferris was taken out, Coin stood so still he didn't feel the pulses of his blood. "Now then," the voice said evenly, "I want you to pick up every book that's off the shelves of this room, straighten the pages, and put them back in their exact places."

Coin was glad he had seen the pictures of the boy and girl in the commander's box and would press them into his mind forever . . . like Woody, Bernice. He went on picking up books, pressing the creased pages flat, retrieving the printed civilization of the world. He placed them in order on the shelves slowly, carefully, in a slow, embarrassed motion. He felt as if he were doing a tortured dance in a library under the sea. He felt the knowledge of the books in his hurt eyes and his thighs, in his chest, in his arm—everywhere Ferris Wing had hit him. Ferris Wing! He had never thought of calling Ferris by both his names but now it made Ferris and all that had happened seem impersonal, just like thinking "Marky" for Lieutenant Commander Mark had made the commander real, as if the Alabama voice coming out of the mouth at the library table were his father's voice. Now he did not want a father but needed one. More than that he needed a friend, and a home. Perhaps like Fortunata's. . . . He wanted to look Marky square in the eye and confess his dreams that emerged from the seashell and the terror that once came from it.

At last there was only one book left, *A Shropshire Lad*. Holding it in his hands, he couldn't help it but one verse stuck in his mind and he said it aloud because at last he knew, by some magic of time, he had not been responsible for what had happened.

Here by the labouring highway
With empty hands I stroll;
Sea-deep, till doomsday morning,
Lie lost my heart and soul.

Coin put the book carefully on a shelf as the commander's voice came back with another verse they had both read aloud:

Now hollow fires burn out to black,
And lights are guttering low:
Square your shoulders, lift your pack,
And leave your friends and go.

He turned to look at that olive-colored, beloved face, decided not to reply and left the library.

Chapter Nine

What in the world was Deaconess Quick doing, perching on a barstool? Coin was startled and delighted to see all her great fat way up on high. A pillar of the church, no less, was on that red artificial leather stool tasting her beer with relish. Well, bless her soul. As he watched her from his distance, she seemed perfectly at home taking small sips and giggling into her glass of beer, lifting the five-cent communion to her purple lips. She didn't look to left or right but worded her head to the mirror in front of her with secret smilings and panting joy. Maybe he should go out before she recognized him. As he started toward the door, the familiar voice hit his back like a syphon spraying him. He turned.

"Coin Foreman, well, now, you know. You mean you weren't going to say the word to me . . . I'm ashamed, honey. Yes, I'm ashamed, you know, that you wouldn't press my heart after all these years. Come here, honey, now you know, and say a word." Coin stood at attention. "I ain't ashamed, honey, I learned long ago about the eat, drink and be merry, which is in the *Bible*, Lord."

The people in the room looked first at Coin and then at her and held their laughter in. She was ridiculous as an Easter hat fashioned of paper roses and colored eggs. That's what she had on, too. And a violet dress flowered with poppies. She looked like a field held on high. And laughed with fat joy. Her bosoms bloomed toward the bar and settled in satisfaction when Coin walked to her. Getting down from the stool she was a parade of flirtation and arthritis. Now she held him in her arms, kissing beer into his cheeks and into his newly pressed uniform. "Home again, home again," she said. He breathed into her old softness. She patted him into childhood and sobbed the past into his chest. "Here he come, a grown man into my arms. Now you know, that's nice. A old lady is blessed to see you, to see thee. Coin, he has returned to me."

Coin tried to break the embrace gently, but Mrs. Quick clung to him like a log in her drowning. "Don't go away, my honey, my dear. Stay with your deaconess for the second, for my time. Now you realize meetings come but the once or twice. Stay with me. Do you reckon we could get a table? I can't climb that stool the second time. Coin, get a table and let's sit us down and talk now you a grown man and *capable*. Now you do that."

Coin got the table and they sat down, the precious past between them suspended and waiting for the belch of her news to spew forth. He ordered new drinks as Deaconess Quick grinned at him foolishly and he grinned back at her. He prepared to stay a while.

"Thanks for this here beer, Coin. These old bones needs cooling in this heat. Ain't it something, though? I just comes here regular and spends a little change. Not much, mind you. But beer nearly as cheap as coffee or tea. I ain't worried about getting fat. Too late for that. Sometimes when I see the young like you, I just want to wind back my time, honey. Set my clock at eighteen years old. You how old?"

"Just about nineteen, Mrs. Quick."

"Then eighteen is my number. The woman, she should always be a step behind the man." She threw back her head and alarmed out laughter. Coin had to laugh with her, she was enjoying herself so much.

"First, let me tell you this. Chile, they tried to put me out of the church. A year ago almost to this hour. Called a meeting of the righteous; they tried to hand my letter back and throw me out like suet, now you know. After all I done nursing the sick and bereaved, working to put my share into them collection plates. Deaconess Redmond, I am surprised at that woman, pointed her finger at me and declared that I had been drinking beer, not only in my home but *also* in a bar. Now Coin, I never took a drink on the Lord's day, not that every day ain't the Lord's day but on Sundays, I mean. I stop my beers on Saturday sharp at twelve midnight and don't commence again till after twelve midnight Sunday night. Now you know, there ain't nothing wrong with that."

Coin had beckoned the waiter for two more beers.

"I told the Deacon and Deaconess Boards that even our Lord turned the water to wine. And you know, now don't you, that wine is stronger than beer? Yes, it is!"

Coin nodded. "Uh, huh."

"And I ain't never disgraced myself in public. That's what I told Deaconess Redmond, and you know what that old fool shouted? 'Don't you, Mrs. Quick (not even my title of deaconess did she use), don't you ever use any word with *grace* in it because you done fell from grace, and all the king's horses nor all of God's men can ever glue you back together again'."

Mrs. Quick was leaning across the table and got confidential, whispering, "Well, after she stomped out, I told the Boards a thing or two, not only about Deaconess Redmond but about a few of themselves. And they shut up like clams and called the meeting to a close. The upshot is and was that I'm still a deaconess and . . ." with this she shook a finger at Coin, reached for her beer and pronounced, "and, I emphasizes, in good standing. That's the truth, just as I'm sitting here, now that's that, please my precious Savior. Thank you for this drink, boy." She drained her glass. Without any warning to Coin, tears began to run down the channels of her cheeks.

"Oh Lord, here I am, a old lady crying in the public eye."

"Mrs. Quick, would you like to go out for some fresh air?"

She snuffed in the tears saying, "No, Coin Foreman, when you get as old as me, you crying one minute and laughing the next, or jest set looking at the past, now you know. Take the time you been away, why things happened so fast, you would've thought you was in some of the moving pictures, they went so crowded and so fast. Lord, I been talking so much. Let me hear your adventures. The picture you sent of that island was pretty as your soul, oh it was! Speaking about events going on. You know that old Italian woman, Mrs. Renaldo, who was always wearing black? Just dropped dead in the streets. Didn't even wait for the coma! They say she had liquor on the breath, too. But that ain't so much to holler about. The police went up into that apartment, now you know what they found? Guess, son."

"Can't think."

"Well, I can tell you it were no sugar and spice. *Tombstone catalogues*, thousands of them, chile. She'd been collecting for years. Some were large as Montgomery Ward and the Sears and Roebuck catalogues. Yellow and peeling. And a little doll, a girl doll she must've thought was real 'cause they found changes of clothes for every description."

Coin had missed Mrs. Renaldo as much as he had missed Mrs. Quick, and his air smelled now of peppermints and Chianti wine and black-dye bosom perspiration. In his mind he saw Mrs. Renaldo's black veils flapping against the doors of all the dead in his past and her past. He was glad that she had dropped dead suddenly, not rotting away while living.

"Let me tell you about dolls, chile. When I was a girl, now you realize that was many years ago, although many a deacon wink at me even now. (Men has got filthy minds, sewer places.) When I was a girl in Mississippi, my white folks gave me two wax dolls. In them days there were no hard and permanent dolls like they got now. I got to loving those children so much, I talked to them like I'm talking to you about just everything.

"One summer those folks who give me them dolls decided to travel, in the heat now, to New Orleans. So naturally when we was packing, I didn't pack no dolls. I was bent and determined that I would carry them personal. My Mama said that there was no room for such foolishness, but I kicked up such a storm they let me take *one*."

Coin said to himself, fart on such foolishness.

"They promised to send the other, crated and in tar paper against the sun. So we traveled on. Of course I was in the jim crow car with the windows open and the hot air blowing in and not a fan going. The hottest day of that July, I fell asleep by a window, cradling that wax in my arms. I woke up in a hot dark sweat. The child's eyes had crossed each other and melted into the cheeks, the pretty, pink dress was all wax and my fat doll had done grown skinny. Blonde hair matted and lips smeared. I was fit to be tied in my own hair ribbons. Now you know, I wept like Jesus in the chapter. I kicked and I fussed. I cried at the foot of the cross.

"Let me tell you what I did when we arrived in New Orleans. Immediately I asked if the twin doll had arrived and it had. It had!"

Mrs. Quick, sh-sh-shhhh, oh shut up.

"The white folks' houseman uncrated the body at once and delivered it to me. I was quiet as Eastertide when I went to the kitchen, frisking my black self, and asked for a knife to cut something or other, I don't remember what lie I told. Went back to the room, now you recognize I did, and took up the second doll and slashed away at her in New Orleans to make sure the same thing wouldn't happen to my second that happened to my first. Couldn't bear to go through the second grief. Ain't that strange?"

"Deaconess Quick, would you like another glass of beer?"

"Honey, I ain't gonna hop around here like a grasshopper, but I accept your offer. Doesn't come too once in a while, this offer, pain come twice or in all numbers but not a treat!" Coin signaled and presently the beer was brought.

"What brand of beer is this?"

"Draft," Coin shouted over the noise and music.

"Draft," she echoed. "One of the best brands there is!"

"Deaconess Quick, is everything OK?"

"OK as the world, and you know how that is?" A calm settled down. For a moment they were silent together. She fished up the last taste of her glass and with arms outstretched and her head bowed on the tables as if it were the altar in the New Corinthian Baptist Church, Mrs. Quick slumped.

"Mrs. Quick, Mrs. Quick!"

"I am," she said as she raised her hand, "a deaconess, not Mrs. Please, Coin, wash Mrs. Redmond and her vicious wart from your mind. Who's gonna wash me white as snow? Wash me in the grace? Nobody." There was a long pause while music raked the air. "Whilst you were away I attended Miss Lucy Horwitz. Who, now you reckon, is laying in the undertaker's, Branton's Morticians, in her deeds? She's laying there and ain't provided a cent for my nurse's care or the laundry of my uniforms, and I was always neat. That shows just how much you can get attached to nothings out of the goodness of your very heart. Now you know, I never loved that woman. She were distressed and I had to help, naturally, as you'd help anybody in distress. . . ."

"What in the world are you saying, Mrs. Quick?"

"Do I have to tell you again? I'm Deaconess. . . ."

"Who," and he held his breath, "who did you say was dead?"

"I want my proper title, do you hear me? I'm a servant of the Lord and I want to be called by my proper title and I ain't gonna say another word till you do." And she sat up righteously and called for another beer. Coin just looked at her while juices of his past life rose in him.

"Deaconess. . . ."

"That's better," she shot back, "now where was I? . . ."

"Somebody just died. . . ."

"*Miss* Lucy Horwitz refused the help of the doctors till the last minute, she refused the help of Jesus *and* His Father and *my* help at the end. She went to her death without the mercy of a coma, screaming inside a straightened jacket and her teeth turned black. . . . The funeral's tomorrow from the Branton's parlor but that's one funeral I need not attend with my smelling salts and ointments because there won't be nobody there to fall out." She drank the rest of her beer in one long gulp and began to straighten her hat and brush her bosom. She lurched to Coin's side.

"Oh, my, Coin Foreman, the world has changed since my day. I ain't got no day no more. Hypocritics and worry is about the whole story, the only thing I can tell my Jesus." The tears started again. "Boy, this beer is something. What the brand again? Draft, Drafts." Her behind pulled her down and Coin only heard her faintly as she called out. "Waiter, waiter. Bring me some Drafts. And bring one for my son, I got my son now. . . ."

199

Coin was walking toward the door as she smiled at his empty chair, saying something that sounded like a drunken prayer. "Death happen only the once to everybody, Coin, ain't that good!" He headed for the bar at Sumner and Quincy to think the news out by himself.

Once in the bar he threw his head on an empty, compassionate table, forced himself to sleep and dreamed:

When the steeple of the Corinthian Baptist Church crashed then the smoke rose up in shapes out of Pandora's box in the pulpit: caterpillar smoke turning to butterflies and moths of gray and black, fogs of eyes spread their looking: bird eyes of vultures, the first robin with the breast of fire; the stars he hadn't seen in his father's sky appeared red and orange and left forever in the mouths of the birds; he began to see his family and friends up there blown about in the heads of birds, whipped like whipped black cream by the wings of smoke animals; there were dogs on fire, cats chasing bait; his father's secret cigar smoked out of his crisp mustache was burning him up; his mother's crepe-paper rose was on fire and there were a million hands that couldn't put it out; his brother Oscar's stinking feet spread dirty jam across all birds, all faces, butterflies and stars; Miss Horwitz's mouth was spread in smoke teeth and smelling up everything; nothing was clean and he itched all over wanting a bath, thinking in a million ways. Oh, this night would never end for him; he was trapped in

*hell in downtown Brooklyn and would never return
to Berriman Street or see his friend, Ferris. Bernice
jumped rope in the smoke, in and out, French style
... that meant double ovals. If he ever escaped
from this he would forgive God and Miss Horwitz;
he would be A-number-one in Sunday School and
real school, he would gather horse manure for the
gardens of Berriman Street, free, and he would
never, never steal from the church collection plate.*

So he rested on the table and half awake and
asleep he tired himself in the dream. Then he
whipped awake. When Mrs. Quick first said Miss
Lucy Horwitz was dead, he refused to believe it. He
had always thought that she would never die, she'd
just funk away. At least that's what he had hoped
for her. There would be that general decay and finally the smell of the odors of evil: like bat's shit
and carnal piss, polluted waters, the underground
flush of sewers, the halitosis of worms, of snakes,
asthmatic dogs, toe jam, uninspected prostitutes,
the devil's armpits, the breath of lice and mayonnaise curdled with maggots; seedy diseases feeding
on the garbage and marrow left in human bones.
The agony she had made his family suffer grew
monumental in the alcoholic fumes of his brain,
and would give him no peace. He fidgeted. She had
tried to destroy all of them each in a different way
but now she was dead in an undertaker's parlor,
still bugging him into drink—and that might bug
him, too.

Determination began to grow in Coin as he

recovered and drank his beers. He had a half pint of blended Green River whiskey in his sock and every once in a while he would go to the room marked *Gents* for another taste. Then all the neurotic bowels of his life began to tell on him before he rushed again to the *Gents*. From upstairs the music made a horror of blanketed noise, a juke box singer whispered in a cosy, noisy song. The urinal flushed noisily. Coin rushed from the room. He had rejected everything and wished he was swimming where fish were small and the water was clean. Lord have mercy, I'm drunk near my own street and lonely as a hill cat. . . . Astonished at himself he left some bills on the bar and rushed out for the funeral parlor at a fast clip. He had had so much to drink that to keep from reeling and rocking, he hugged his toes in and began to march to a tune the sailors used to sing to keep in step:

You had a good home but you left,
You left. You had a good home but you left,
Left. . . .

He leaned against the nearest lamppost and doubled over in ironic laughter. He couldn't stand laughing; his stomach screwed up in a hard ball. Chile, you're on the streets, pull yourself together. "You left!" he shouted into the light overhead. "You left like shit, you were put out, dispossessed, thrown into the tangles of the world at seventeen."

202

The lines of his mind grew taut; the ball in his stomach began to bounce and he hugged the lamppost like Mary, in those Italian pictures, folding Jesus in her arms. His world had seemed so wide and open before his sister died. Now he had seen the world, some of it leastaways, and he recognized what life could be and was. He was only in his first semester of hope and grief, and here he was marching back to the last death. He wished that he had something to fold in his arms other than this iron post with light at the top to search out evil in the streets.

You had a good home but you left,
You left. . . .

He began tramping out the song, still hugging the iron searchlight; around him night was flapping a black-blue flag of truce. He knew that he had to go to the dead enemy of his youth, dead and invulnerable to the agony of the unheard taunts, threats, accusations. Ha, ha, death always happened to somebody else, not the dead. He loosed himself and proceeded down the street with nothing in his arms to hold. He felt free now, walking to the end that had bugged him. But there was no fear in his staggering.

You had a good home but you left,
You left, left. . . .

The dirty old bitch, dilapidated hag. Home! Shit, no. It was a house. A bent house. He never wanted to lay eyes on it again.

Tipping his sailor's cap at a rakish angle, he entered the funeral home. Home! It sure is her home now. The final horizontal home. . . .

Amber bulbs, shaped like flame, lit the entrance way. The smell of death hit him. From some unseen source a record was playing "Nearer My God to Thee." The record was cracked and at each turn the music bumped and hissed and scratched its way on through the dust of hundreds of weeping wakes held in this damp, leaky room where it seemed no sun ever came, where the spirit of God had never dwelt. Whoever was buried from this place was bound for someplace just as dilapidated, funky and hot as hell must be. The thought cheered him up a little. He sure smelled his beer, as if he had been washed in it. Beer and death on the breath. He laughed. "Nearer my God to Thee (click, hiss, scratch), nearer to Thee."

There was a stand near the door with a sign over it: *Visitors Please Sign Here.* He didn't hesitate but whipped out his pen and obliged. He wrote in large, clean letters: COIN FOREMAN WAS HERE. Let her put that in her pipe and smoke it. Those words preached a sermon to the wicked. He winked to himself. There were hardly any other names in the book. "Few have come to call," he whispered to himself as he approached the cheap oak coffin.

The grain was large and vulgar, the stain was

cheap and still smelled, the lining was low-grade
rayon sewn in gathers, making it appear that the
body was lying in whipped cream. The light on the
upturned lid sent out rays the color of forty-nine-
cent sherry. She had given orders to save on her
burial. Death wouldn't get any more of her hard-
earned money than necessary. She might need it in
the sweet bye and bye. He tilted his hat forward
and hiked his pants. He noticed a wreath of pink
and white gladioli on the lower part of the casket.
(Pink and white: the colors of spring, the colors of
virgins, colors of innocence, affection, love, soft
colors of ladies in gardens, colors of houses in
southern Italy where children were abundant and
laughter was ready.) There were secondhanded
flowers from a Negro florist who bought the last
and the least and sold them to secondhanded
people: the last and the least.

A real joy shot through him as he moved closer.
He would not take his hat off. Not to her. In a way
he was shocked that she had never loved him but
had used him and his inheritance; had gotten rid of
him to fulfill a perverted affection for his sister
which, he was sure, was never consummated. Perhaps that was why she was so bitter, was determined to destroy as much joy for others as possible,
since joy or even crumbs of happiness would never
come to her. Agnes's great simplicity, like his
mother's, led her to trust the vultures and the bright
snakes of this world—thinking that because they
were God's creatures they couldn't be truly treach-

erous. Miss Lucy Horwitz had never known the geography of natural love or cared for it. No one had ever charted the courses of her body. She was a vagabond to love who tested where she was tolerated but had never sat down to a full meal. Didn't dare to. For all her hardness, she had been a coward. She had been a destroyer. On his ship last year in hours off he had read the *Inferno*, but Dante's hell was a literary one and understandable; the hell Lucy had created was not to be believed by anyone but him. All her victims were dead.

No. He would not take his hat off. He had learned that much: not to bow to the destroyer, even in death. Death was not so much. Anyway, it had its own immaculateness beyond all his potential courtesy. So he moved closer, still wearing his racked hat. The beer came riding up in him like love and destruction. He was in a sudden panic and turned around swiftly to find a hiding place. Instead he reached into his sock for his half pint. There were faint noises overhead and smells seemed to ride about the room in waves: bacon frying, chitlins, greens. A sudden crash of dishes brought him to. They're probably drunk up there, too. Who wouldn't be, living with the dead forever in your parlor? There was a frantic rolling overhead and a dog began to howl. And then the barking of human voices, fighting, stoning each other with words. Well, at least, Miss Horwitz was in her usual environment. Death couldn't steal her away from that.

As he looked down into the sliced mouth of her

death, he saw that she was really dead in the virgin green of her shroud. Shriveled up in whipped cream. She was as gone as a snuffed-out cigar and the color of one. She looked chewed up, cancerous, utterly finished. She looked hard as pavement. He whispered: *Mene, Mene Tekel Upharsin.* She was dead after all. He took another big swig and standing ten feet tall, in a porous of joy, he spat the whole drink in her dead face. What was left in the bottle he poured over that mouth, on those hands that had commanded him as a child, at puberty, in adolescence. Then he tossed the bottle in her stingy coffin; without staggering, he left the foul funeral parlor like a man.

Chapter Ten

Coin walked down Pennsylvania Avenue and turned into Fulton Street. There was hardly any traffic or people. The El trains roared overhead at regular intervals like ordered thunder. He crossed into the middle of the street. On either side of him the great iron posts were his guards. He went on ahead, not really knowing where he was going, but feeling that he was being drawn to some destination, that if he tried to turn back, his way would lead to the funeral parlor again. If Bernice had been with him earlier, he wondered how she would have acted. Would she have screamed curses and stamped as she relived the times when she and Miss Lucy scratched each other with emotional barbed wire? Or would she have stood there and policed her soul in triumphant patience. It was hard to tell about Bernice. You can become attached even to the enemy and feel lost without domestic wars.

Coin remembered the time when there hadn't

been a fuss in the house for almost two months. All had been peaches and cream. So the day before Miss Lucy's birthday (Bernice declared that she was older than Plymouth Rock), Agnes suggested that they have a birthday dinner. She'd cook the meal and Bernice could bake the cake. Bernice went at it with a will. She even bought extra eggs with her own money and used a cook book to make sure it would turn out extra right. When the cake was finished and decked out in pink icing, Bernice smiled with satisfaction at Agnes and Coin and Woody. "How many candles, Agnes?" Bernice asked. Agnes giggled. Then she got herself together and said almost like Popa: "I think 'Happy Birthday to Miss Lucy' in another color icing will suffice." They all laughed like happy conspirators and Bernice went about the business.

Coin had suggested earlier that they eat in the back garden. He and Woody brought out the table and chairs and set up. At the last minute Bernice ran out and bought balloons. They blew them up, attached them to sticks and planted them in the grass all over. Blue and yellow and red and white and orange, purple, green. The balloons nodded to each other in the breeze. The air was merry with color.

When Miss Lucy arrived they sang "Happy Birthday to You." She went out to the garden with them. Her face was stiff throughout the whole meal, although she ate aplenty. When Bernice brought in the cake Miss Lucy glanced at Agnes and everyone glanced at her. Coin held his breath. "I think you ought to cut it," Agnes said brightly. Miss Lucy took the knife Agnes handed her and proceeded to cut the slices. She took up her fork. Bernice watched her. Miss Lucy tasted. Coin could see that she thought it was good, but she turned to Agnes after she had taken her first bite and said, "Yes, yes, but something's missing, Agnes."

She glanced sideways at Bernice.

Agnes said out loud, "Lucy, I think it's wonderful. Maybe the best cake I ever tasted, don't you think so?" Coin noticed the quiet show of tears in Bernice's eyes. Then they came down slowly and dissolved into the piece before her.

"Too many eggs perhaps." Coin knew that Miss Lucy was making a joke to hide her embarrassment at being the center of the show. He also knew that Bernice didn't sense this. Suddenly Bernice rammed her chair back, swiftly took a bobby pin from her hair, and like a jumping jack, like wild Bill from the island, she went from balloon to balloon and stuck each one. There were yellow pops, and blue and green, and pops of all the colors of balloons in the garden. Bernice was crying all the while. And when she saw the last balloon—red—it was right at Miss Lucy's chair. She went over with deliberate haste and punched. The balloon wrinkled down red. The wind blew the thin rubber against Miss Lucy's dress. Everyone was still. Suddenly Miss Lucy went over to Bernice, lifted her tear-filled face, looked at her for a long, long, suspense time and then hugged her. They were both crying. "Why, Bernice," she said in a voice of flowers, "I've never had my birthday celebrated. Thank you. Thank you." Then she walked into the house. Coin noticed that she was crying with the rest of them.

Perhaps Bernice would be at the funeral tomorrow. That was the only reason he might go. He looked at the color of the night. It was the curious deep gray-purple of Concord grapes. The thunder of the trains roared overhead and he walked past stations. Now he passed the Cumberland stop and was on his way to Lafayette. He felt clear and alive, and in some way those great iron posts that were his guards made him feel mystical. He almost felt as though he were walking in a procession: dark and ritual and Italian. Any hangover he had expected had not come. Two trains thundered over, going in opposite directions, and as they crossed overhead in a lightning burst, Miss Lucy appeared to him. She sculptured herself on an iron post ahead. He had to move magnetlike toward her, pinioned and suspended, with her basement bargain shroud, stiff and second rate. He had to pass her and, bless God, he did. He was surprised how easy it was. She was dead. Ha, ha. Death had delivered him from fighting. But if he had to fight again, when he first recognized the enemy, he would put on the armor of his new awareness, his courage, his total aloneness, and wrestle like Jacob to win without the help of any human creature or of death. He was learning slowly what his past had meant; perhaps what he was to become.

The next station was almost above him. He proceeded under thunder beside the tall iron guards. He began to think of the stations of the cross that he had seen in a thousand churches of Italy—of the devotion that had put them there and of the centuries of women who had prayed before them.

Stations of the cross! He was far from those stations in the churches of Rome and Venice and Florence, Verona, Naples, Ravenna, Capri, Ischia, far from Fortunata's church where the Gloria amazed with doves and colored bits of paper on Easter morning.

He was at a station all right: Ralph Avenue in Brooklyn, New York. He had started walking from Pennsylvania and Fulton. How many stations had he passed? He had begun to play a game. Not a game to amuse himself or to pass the time while he was drawn forward, but a game of following the Jesus Christ of his fathers and of Fortunata's people in his pilgrim's progress up Fulton Street.

He suddenly felt a little drunk but he would be all right if he matched his Brooklyn stations with the stations of the cross. And to hell with Miss Lucy! Hell. Miss Lucy wasn't in Heaven he knew. She was in Hell. She had to be there. He hoped not. He wanted her plain dead with no retribution or anything, just dead. If she was in Hell he would die one day and meet her there. That would be too much. Let her just be plain dead and nowhere. Ha ha, ho ho, me laddie O! Where were Lieutenant Commander Mark and poetry? Ralph Avenue . . . he had passed that. No, this was Reid Avenue station. The thunder train roared overhead. He was at station number four: *Jesus Meets His Afflicted Mother*, at Reid Avenue and Fulton. Mama, Mama, Mama, take my Mama home. His Mama was home but he was walking. She was home . . . home. He had no home. He walked along until he got to Troy.

Troy Avenue station: *Jesus Consoles the Weeping Women of Jerusalem*. He remembered when Reverend Brooks had preached a sermon at June graduation and spoke directly to the Negro mothers in the congregation. "You have," he said, "washed the white folks' floors and cooked their million dinners, kept their family together while your husbands wandered from Jerusalem, you have darned socks and washed underwear and praised the Lord to put your children through school, praise your souls, praise your sweet time, praise the grease of your elbows and the stout muscles of your hearts."

Old Sister Burroughs, who had not only put her children through high school but also her grandchildren, shot up out of her pew and raised a black and bony fist upward to her God and shouted: "Yes, I did it, yes, I did it, yes, I did it." She danced in dedication and fainted into Deacon Loring's fat arms.

Coin strode along. The gray-purple of Concord

grapes in the sky had turned to eggplant color. The streets were completely deserted. At Tompkins Avenue station *Jesus Fell the Third Time* and at Nostrand, *He Was Stripped of His Garments and the Soldiers Played Dice* for his immortal clothes. Coin still pushed forward with the iron guards fixed to guide his magnet traveling.

As he neared Franklin Avenue, *Jesus Died on the Cross and Three Women Wept for Him*. Mama, Agnes, and Mrs. Quick. He walked two more stations: *Jesus Was Taken Down from the Cross*. Lieutenant Commander Mark was Simon, the Cyrene; he helped Joseph of Arimathea and the others do it. Then he yanked up the cross and carried it over every hill of Calvary and the others until he disappeared.

When he reached Lafayette Avenue station: *Jesus Was Laid in the Tomb,* John and the three women, Mary, Martha, and Mary Magdalen, were walking away, beyond grief: their miracle friend was dead. Jesus was carried by the thieves: Ferris and the shadow Horace followed by Miss Lucy into the stony sepulcher where they laid him down and threw the nails in the crevices of his shroud and poppies began to grow at once where bandages held him tightest.

Coin turned into the street that led into Fort Greene Park and climbed to the lookout where he had seen his church burn down on a sour night almost nine years before. He had to laugh a little at his imagination; who did he think he was, anyway,

Jesus Christ? There was no answer for that. What did stations of the cross and stations of Brooklyn and Italian women and Negro mothers have to do with all the mess of Miss Lucy's dying and his living? A few minutes ago at station twelve, Vanderbilt Avenue, the image of Jesus talking to His Father was appealing to him. But not now. The Savior's cold, lone figure lying stretched in the dark, mumbling the seven last words to His Father, was not for him, was not for him, not yet. But he knew that he would never try the way of Ferris or of Miss Lucy Horwitz. Easy ways and dark ways would not tempt him. Maybe that was why Christ kept looming up on his journey: to make the lesson of the sacrifice of the cross wrap him around like the weather of his mother's life.

The rumbling of the trains filled his stomach and he wished he hadn't drunk so much. Before he realized it he was climbing up to the lookout in Fort Greene Park. Below him was the New Corinthian Baptist Church, rebuilt in a modern design. It thrust itself up in a hulk rather than a spire of faith—but that was all right. The body of a church was there. His father had practically died pronouncing it, collecting money for it, dreaming of his funeral in it, but the foundation had only been dug when he died.

Coin shivered as he looked at the night around him. The air had become darker and misty, the stars seemed to have a caul over them; the moon had moved behind a cloud. There was no hint of

216

sound anywhere. Only a few early birds hopped without chirping. A black cat ran like moving night. He turned his body the other way on the bench so that the cat wouldn't cross in front of him. He couldn't afford bad luck. Not now, Jesus, not now. There was a flutter in the stillness at his feet, and he imagined the rats of time whirring in the earth. There was a moving in the air like suspended, transparent worms. He sat extra still in the magic stillness. Now not a rat or a cat or a grass or a worm stirred, not a car-honk or a house-sneeze or a padded footfall or a fire siren sounded. And he thought to himself, this is one morning the stars won't sing together; one morning when the church bells won't ring the hours in. The feeling that trembled through his body was frightening because he couldn't define it. He knew somebody or thing was approaching him. But he could see nothing. Every bit of feeling seemed to be concentrated in that part of his left arm where *DEATH* was tattooed. His arm itched and burned and he couldn't lift a hand to scratch. Maybe he was asleep. He shut his eyes tight, then opened them quickly. Bernice was there in front of him.

"Hello, kiddo," she said, "you're up pretty late, aren't you?"

Coin stared at her. The burning in his arm stopped.

"I just heard about Miss Lucy tonight," she continued. "I had a hunch you'd be here so I got up out of my bed and came right over. Aren't you glad to see me after all this time? It wasn't easy to get out tonight, I can tell you."

At last Coin could speak.

"Of course I'm glad to see you. Jesus, I'm glad as hell to see you."

Bernice chuckled. "Watch out mixing Jesus and Hell."

"You haven't changed a bit," Coin answered, and they laughed together like in the old times. Suddenly she was serious. "You're grown up. I never thought I'd see you grown. You're looking good, too. Say, what have you been drinking? It smells terrible."

"Well," he answered, "Deaconess Quick and I had more rounds than you can shake a stick at."

Bernice roared. "Well, well, well," she kept saying, "well, well, well."

"I wouldn't stand in your way if you wanted a drink."

"You couldn't," was all she could say through her laughter.

"Say, Bernice, seriously, where are you living? Could you put me up for a few days . . . I haven't any place, you know, no home or anything until my furlough is up."

"In the first place, you wouldn't like where I'm living and in the second place, the place is too small and I couldn't get you in even if I wanted to. But one of these days, kiddo. . . ."

"Yes, Bernice. . . ." He wanted her to say that

218

when he got out of the navy they'd find a place together.

She looked at him out of the corners of her eyes. Coin noticed that she was crying. "Now why did you go and bring up . . ." she hesitated, "living . . . you mean together?" She bit her lower lip.

Quickly Coin said, "I just thought it would be nice since we're both alone."

"It's impossible so forget it." They were both silent for a moment and she said suddenly, "I saw Miss Lucy tonight, she looked a mess."

"You went to the funeral parlor? I didn't see your name on the register!"

Bernice just gave a low chuckle.

Coin faced her. "You're full of jokes tonight."

She answered, "Oh, it's just that I'm so glad to be out, even for a minute."

"You mean away from your family . . . your husband and the baby."

"Say, look, Coin, I haven't any family, we never married but the baby's with me. Now I've said it and now you know."

"I'm, I'm sorry. Damn sorry."

"Don't be sorry for me, Coin. I loved that man. I loved him and I had his child. It was a cute girl. . . ."

" 'Was,' I thought you said she was with you . . . ?" Coin was confused.

"You don't understand, you couldn't. But look, before I go I want you to understand that everything is fine with me. Fine. And you . . . you have a time. And now that you've got nobody and are free you can start over fresh and make your life what you want it to be. Don't think about Miss Lucy or what she did. She's dead, thank God, dead. Erase her from your mind. I'm glad you were here tonight, Coin. I've got to go now, I've got to go before the bells ring, good-bye, good sweet, bye and bye, good-bye." And she backed away looking at him and then turned and ran. Coin ran after her. He heard her calling back to him loud and assuring, as if she were yelling on Berriman Street: "I'll tell everybody you're all right."

"Bernice, Bernice, Bernice. . . ." When he got to the west end of the lookout she had disappeared. She was nowhere to be seen. She couldn't have gone anywhere except forward, but where was she? Where was she? "Bernice!" He thought he'd yell his lungs out. "Bernice, Bernice."

His head hit the back of the bench. His hat fell off. He saw the church before him. The clocks of the churches of Brooklyn began chiming five o'clock. A few cars honked in the distance. He heard an alarm clock go off. A few birds began to sing in perfect unison. They stopped. Slowly he picked up his hat and brushed it off automatically, straightened the wrinkles of his uniform, automatically, put his cap on, automatically. He took up his ditty bag with the seashell and the graduation book of signatures and slung it over one shoulder. The sun came up slowly to prepare the day. He looked up and smiled, saying: "I heard from my sister last night." He was young, facing life, without the roll-call of those he loved: Mama, Popa, Agnes, Bernice (where in the world was Woody?); even without the enemy: Lucy Horwitz. The sun came totally up, making Brooklyn rosy and the sky high and bright. He began to walk. He felt into his pocket for the stone Fortunata had given him, the stone that shone in the dark, and rolled it in his pocket. He felt his father's watch ticking time against his heart. As he passed the place Bernice had disappeared, in his mind he heard her singing:

Come home early, chile,
Come home early, chile,
Come home early, chile,
And I'll rock you in my arms.

He listened for a moment at the edge of the lookout and then turned away and took the nearest path into the bright city.

THE END

National Bestsellers
from Popular Library

☐	THE HOLLOW MOUNTAINS—Oliver B. Patton	$1.95
☐	THE LANDLADY—Constance Rauch	$1.75
☐	NINE MONTHS IN THE LIFE OF AN OLD MAID Judith Rossner	$1.50
☐	THE BEST PEOPLE—Helen Van Slyke	$1.75
☐	THE CAESAR CODE—Johannes M. Simmel	$1.95
☐	THE HEART LISTENS—Helen Van Slyke	$1.75
☐	TO THE PRECIPICE—Judith Rossner	$1.75
☐	THE COVENANT—Paige Mitchell	$1.95
☐	TO KILL A MOCKINGBIRD—Harper Lee	$1.50
☐	COMPANIONS ALONG THE WAY—Ruth Montgomery	$1.75
☐	THE WORLD BOOK OF HOUSE PLANTS—E. McDonald	$1.50
☐	WEBSTER'S NEW WORLD DICTIONARY OF THE AMERICAN LANGUAGE	$1.75
☐	WEBSTER'S NEW WORLD THESAURUS	$1.25
☐	THE LAST CATHOLIC IN AMERICA—J. R. Powers	$1.50
☐	THE HOUSE PLANT ANSWER BOOK—E. McDonald	$1.50
☐	INTRODUCTION TO TERRARIUMS Barbara Joan Grubman	$1.50
☐	A BRIDGE TOO FAR—Cornelius Ryan	$1.95
☐	THE LONGEST DAY—Cornelius Ryan	$1.75
☐	THE LAST BATTLE—Cornelius Ryan	$1.95
☐	FEAR AND LOATHING IN LAS VEGAS Dr. H. S. Thompson	$1.75